Jenna's Journey

Steven Lake

Published by Steven Lake, 2015.

Table of Contents

Jenna's Journey

By Steven Lake
Smashwords Edition

Author's Introduction

Jenna's Journey is a short novel told from a unique two part perspective. The first is the events of the story told from the viewpoint of the supportive, and secondary characters who play an important part in the experiences of the main character. The second is the story retold, but this time from the viewpoint of the main character. With this you get a unique perspective on the entirety of this wonderful adventure as seen from "both sides of the aisle", so to speak. I originally wrote this book as an experiment after being challenged by my friends to write a story using this unique, two party writing style, and I have to say that I was quite thrilled with the outcome. As such, I hope that you will enjoy reading this book just as much as I did writing it. And now, we begin the story.

Prologue

Margaret, a Godly woman and long time owner of the wonderful, albeit obscure, Shepherds Bed and Breakfast, just off Highway 28, had finished her work for the day, and was finally laying down to rest, long after her evening's guests had themselves gone to bed. However, unlike in times past, the bed felt unusually large to her; many, many times bigger than she would ever need for herself. This was because, several months earlier, her husband had passed away, leaving behind a large void in her life. The emptiness of his side of the bed made her loneliness feel all that much stronger. She gently laid her hand on her husband's empty pillow and thought longingly about her now dearly departed knight of utmost chivalry. He'd been a very loving man, doting on her every day. But now he was gone, resting comfortably in the arms of Jesus, while she continued to maintain the B&B they'd built together.

She sighed slightly, wondering why God had left her behind while taking her husband away at a time when she could really use him the most. It wasn't that she didn't have help, as she had several employees assisting her with the daily duties. It was instead his absence that bothered her the most. It'd caused her, on many an occasion, to long for Heaven even more than before. But, if she was still here, and Jesus hadn't taken her home yet, then there must still be work for her to do. The only question now was, what? Just then, this thought having no more than passed through her mind, she felt the presence of the Lord descend upon her like a warm blanket as a still, small voice echoed in her mind.

"Margaret," it said with great love.

"Lord, is that You?" she asked quietly.

"It is," came a soft, gentle reply.

Margaret's heart leapt within her!

"Speak, Lord, for your servant listens," she replied.

"I have work for you to do."

This is exactly what Margaret wanted to hear!

"What kind of work, Lord?" she asked.

"I am sending a young woman and her children to you. Through you I will give them yet another new beginning. You are to nurture them as your own, for they will come to you with nothing, seeking to start their lives over again. Take good care of them."

"Yes, Lord. I will," replied Margaret.

She pondered this briefly, trying to wrap her mind around this rather unusual assignment, and all that it would entail.

"When will they arrive?" she asked after a moment.

"I will tell you when it is time. Until then, you are to prepare for their needs."

"Yes, Lord, I will. But..."

Margaret heard a soft, loving chuckle greet her incomplete sentence.

"What is it, child?" came the Lord's knowing reply.

"You said this would be *another* new beginning for them. Did they have...well, one before this?"

"They are your new brother and sisters," replied the Lord with a smile.

Margaret's eyes lit up.

"Oh," she said in wonder. "Praise you, Lord! Then they've gained a new life in the spiritual, and now You're giving them a new life in the physical?"

"I am," replied the Lord.

Margaret smiled at this as she sighed happily.

"Thank you, Lord, for this opportunity to minister to this family, and I will do for them all that You have asked of me."

And with that the presence of the Lord lifted from her. Margaret then rolled over and lay quietly on her pillow smiling. There *was* a reason God had left her behind. She still had work to do, and what a work it would be!

Part 1 – The Actors
Scene 1: The Shadow Wall

John awoke with a start, his body sweating as he panted heavily and tried to get his wits about him. His wife rolled over next to him and looked at her husband curiously. By the look on his face she thought he'd seen a ghost.

"What's the matter, dear?" she asked.

"I just had a dream," he said.

His wife sat up on one arm and looked at him curiously.

"What kind?" she asked.

"It was strange, and sorta hyper realistic."

"What was it about?"

"It began with me looking at a map of the country that lay spread out across my desk. As I was studying it, the map seemed to grow larger and larger until I was floating just above our town. As I was watching this, trying to understand what I was seeing, a line appeared on the western horizon, passed through our town, and then disappeared into the east. I then found myself standing in front of a hotel. I think it was the La Quinta Inn downtown. To my right was a car with a small family in it. They wanted to get into the hotel, but they were being blocked by a thick wall of darkness that spread out in front of the building. It prevented them from getting near the door, or approaching the hotel in any way."

"What did it look like? The darkness, I mean. Well, besides being dark, obviously."

John screwed up his face slightly, uncertain of how to describe it.

"I don't know. It was like a curtain of black that was solid and impenetrable."

His wife thought about this briefly.

"Then what happened?" she asked.

"An angel came to me and told me that, for them to enter, I would have to open the door for them. I asked how I was to do that seeing that the wall was impenetrable. He told me that I would need to get a key from within. I argued with him, insisting relentlessly that the wall was impassable. But he told me to go inside anyways, to the main desk, and ask for a key. Eventually I obeyed. To my surprise, I suddenly found myself inside the hotel staring at the front desk. Behind it stood a man dressed head to toe in brown khakis. He said, 'May I help you?' I told him I needed a key. He smiled and handed me a golden key, which I then took outside and gave to the family I'd seen earlier. They were very happy to get it."

His wife smiled.

"Wow, that's great! What happened next?" she asked with almost the same giddy enthusiasm as a young school girl.

"Well, the family took the key I'd just given them and walked up to the hotel. As they did the key began to glow, causing the darkness to melt away, which allowed them to pass through the wall and go inside. But then the wall of darkness turned and came after me. It chased me down and took my wallet. That's when I woke up."

His wife seemed intrigued by this. It was rare enough for her husband to have any dreams at all, let alone one like this.

"Do you think this is from God?" she asked.

"I don't know. I'm not sure what to think of it."

"Then go back to sleep. If it's of God, you'll know," she said.

John laid back down and quickly fell asleep. But the same dream kept playing out in his mind over and over again, repeatedly disturbing his sleep until he couldn't stand it any longer. Finally he got up and went downstairs where he prayed about it until morning, asking God what he should do and what the dream meant. Later that day at work one of his coworkers, a fellow Christian, stopped at John's desk and noticed his friend's tired eyes and clearly troubled countenance.

"Something eating you?" he asked.

"I don't know. I had this really weird dream last night. It kept coming to me over and over again. I'm not sure what to make of it," replied John.

The man turned and poured his entire attention into his friend.

"Tell me more. What was the dream about?" he asked.

John then proceeded to explain everything to his friend. The coworker scratched his chin in interest. John could see the gears grinding in his friend's head and became curious.

"Do you know what it means?" he asked.

"Well, I might. I'll say right up front that dream interpretation is not my forte. However, I'm pretty sure I know what this one is saying."

"And?" asked John.

"Well, when it comes to dreams, objects in the dream can be either one of two things: They can be literal, meaning they're actually trying to get into a real hotel, or they can be symbolic, meaning the hotel is representative of a place of safety or shelter. In this case, however, I'm going to say that this is a blend of the two, with both figurative and literal elements coming together to provide both a narrative on what will happen, and a guide to what things you should do," said the friend thoughtfully.

"So which is which?" asked John.

"Well, my guess would be, the family and the hotel are real, but the wall of darkness is only symbolic. Perhaps the devil, or some unscrupulous individual, is trying to block them from finding shelter in the hotel you saw in the dream. That would be my understanding of it, anyways."

John scratched his chin curiously.

"That's possible. But how will I know that for certain?"

"Well, let me ask you a question. If you had to, could you remember who they were and what they looked like? As in, you'd be able to identify them if you saw them in real life?"

John nodded.

"Yeah, I remember the car, the family, the plate, everything. It was just as real as you and me standing here right now."

"Good, that's the first sign that it was from God. Now, do you remember where you saw the car sitting at?"

"It was in front of the hotel."

The man shook his head.

"Yes, but that's where you'd be wrong. Think about the dream more."

"What do you mean I'm wrong? We were in front of the hotel!" protested John.

The man raised a finger, and replied, "Actually, you weren't. Remember how you said that there was a wall of darkness in front of the hotel that prevented them from getting close to it, or entering? That tells me they weren't actually as close to it as you think."

John thought about this for a bit.

"Alright, so let's assume that you're right, and they weren't actually near the hotel. Then where were they? Or where were *we* for that matter?"

"Well? What else do you remember from the dream? Any environmental sights, sounds, smells, etc?"

John thought about this for a bit. Suddenly a flash of memory echoed in his mind.

"Gas! I remember smelling gas!"

"And...."

"There's a gas station not far from the hotel! Well, the real one, anyways."

The coworker smiled.

"There you go. When you saw them, they were probably at the gas station. Now, one more question. What was on the license plate? You said you remember that."

John pondered this briefly.

"Well, oddly enough, it said 'Barton', almost like it was a vanity plate," he said.

"Any particular state?" asked the friend.

"It was a California plate."

The coworker furrowed his brow.

"Alright then, call me silly, but I'm willing to bet that the letters on the plate are probably their last name rather than actual plate numbers. Evidently someone named Barton from California will be at that gas station at some point in the near future needing a room at the hotel you saw in the dream. But, due to circumstances beyond their control, they will be unable to get inside, and you're supposed to somehow help them," he said.

John crossed his arms and leaned back slightly.

"Hmm, that's possible. But why would they be barred from entering? I know that black fog thing was blocking their path in the dream, but it didn't block me. Therefore it can't be literal. So what do you think it represents?"

The coworker mulled this over for a bit, but couldn't figure out what. Then an idea came to him.

"What was the condition of the car?" he asked.

"It was an older vehicle. I'm not sure the make or model, but it looked something like an old Dodge or Chrysler out of the late 80's."

"And you said you'd be able to identify it if you saw it, right?"

John nodded.

"Yeah, clear as day. Why?"

The coworker pursed his lips slightly.

"Well, this might sound crazy, but I think God was telling you to help someone get a hotel for the night, who otherwise couldn't afford it, while at the same time showing you *who* it was you're being asked to help, and even the specific means by which you're supposed to do it. I say that because of the clarity and specificity of the dream."

John pondered this briefly.

"Okay, I can accept that. But who would it be, and when would they be here?"

"Given that He wouldn't let you sleep last night, I'd say that He's trying to express an urgency to this situation, as though they'll be arriving here sometime tonight."

John looked at his friend in surprise.

"You sure about that!?" he asked.

"God kept giving you the same dream over and over again, didn't He?"

John nodded.

"Yeah, He did, and I didn't get any rest because of it," he replied.

"Then I think you need to go take care of this today."

"But, what if I'm wrong? I'd look like an idiot. Or worse yet, some creepy stalker. I mean, what are people going to think when I show up at a gas station and hand some random person a key to a hotel room?" protested John.

"And what if I'm right and you don't act? Remember the story of Esther? Mordecai told her that she was put into power for just such a time and place, and if she didn't act, God would destroy her and her family, and bring salvation to the Jews through another person. I think the same could be said of you. God has given you so much. Now it's time to make good on those blessings and do this important thing that God has asked of you. If you don't, God may take away all that He's given you and use someone else to do the work instead. So? Will you obey His calling, and risk looking like a fool, or do you want to play it safe and possibly lose everything you have?"

This hit John between the eyes like a hammer.

"No. I'll do it. If I'm wrong, at least I'll be doing it with the right intentions," he said.

The coworker smiled.

"That's all that matters."

John smiled sheepishly in return. He still wasn't sure about this. But, if God was calling him to do this, then he'd do it, no matter what. So, after work, he climbed into his truck, drove downtown, and went into the local La Quinta Inn.

"Hi, I'd like to rent a room for the night," he said to the lady behind the desk.

"Name?" she replied.

"Um, well, I'm paying for the room, but it's going to be used by a family coming in from out of town, if that's alright."

"Their names?" she said without skipping a beat.

John thought back about what his friend had said.

"Barton."

"First name?"

"I'm not sure."

The lady looked at him incredulously.

"You're not sure?" she said in disbelief.

John shrugged.

"Well, I'm not certain which of the Bartons are going to be here, so I don't know whose name to put it under. Can you just put it under the last name and leave it at that?"

She studied him with muted incredulity, and then continued with the check-in process.

"Cash, check or credit?" she asked.

"Credit, please. Oh, and can you add a complimentary dinner onto that?"

"For how many?"

John shrugged.

"Three? I don't know. Can you make it so that whatever they need is charged to my card, including the room and everything else regardless of how much it costs?"

The lady at the desk stared at him mutely for several moments before looking back down at her terminal.

"We can do that if you want," she eventually replied.

John nodded.

"Yes, please do."

He then handed his card to the clerk, who quickly swiped it through the card reader, and handed it back to him. After several more questions, and half a dozen other steps, she handed him two digital key cards.

"Your room is number 117. Would you like standard or express checkout?"

"What's the difference?"

"Standard, you come down here to check out. Express, it checks you out automatically at 11am. So all you have to do is leave and we handle the rest."

"Um, yes, then I'd like express for them, please."

The woman did a few more things with her terminal, and then handed him a form to fill out and sign. Once he'd completed it he handed it back to her. She smiled.

"Thank you, and I hope your friends enjoy their stay at the La Quinta Inn."

John thanked her, and then slipped out of the building. By now he was one step short of having a nervous breakdown, and even less confident that he was making the right decision. In some ways he felt as though this was just one big fat goose chase. He sighed slightly at this, climbed into his truck, and headed down the road towards his home. But, just as he did, a thought crossed his mind. The gas station. If this were real, and he'd actually heard from God, then he'd find them there. Or, if not right away, then very soon. Especially since it was getting towards dusk. So he made his way over to the gas station near the hotel and parked. He then sat there for over an hour waiting, and waiting, and waiting, but there was no sign of the car he'd seen in his dream. This caused the doubt in his mind to grow even larger and stronger. Just then a knock came at his window. To his surprise he saw two young men standing just outside his truck door. Both men had goatees, piercings and tattoos of all kinds scattered across their bodies, and a look of evil in their eyes as though he were staring the Devil in the face. One of the men then pointed a small caliber pistol at him.

"Get out, punk. Now!" he shouted at John.

John carefully climbed out of the truck and held his hands in the air. The one without the gun then walked up to him, rifled through his pockets and took his phone, his wallet, his watch, and anything else of value on him as the other prepared to take his truck. Just then a police car came into the gas station, saw the robbery in progress, and immediately turned on its lights and blared its siren causing the two men to panic and sprint to their car, dropping everything they'd taken from him except his wallet. Wheels screamed, bullets flew, and the chase was on as the two cars raced down the street and into the darkness of the night. John stood there shell shocked, hands still in the air, not sure what to think or do next.

He soon realized that, of all the things they'd taken from him, only his wallet was missing. The rest had been left behind. He then thought about the dream. The darkness. His wallet had been taken. Suddenly believing, for the first time since receiving the dream, that God had really sent him on this mission, his actions didn't seem quite so foolish anymore, nor did his friend's interpretation. Just then a car, looking exactly like the one in his dream, right down to the last nick, dent, and splotch of rust, pulled into the station. John's jaw hit the ground. He put his hands down and stood there watching as the driver got out, filled up with gas, and then went inside to pay.

"Lord, is this them? Is this really the ones you wanted me to help?" he thought.

But God didn't answer. In fact, it felt as though he'd just asked the obvious and had been ignored because of it. As his pastor once said, there's nothing that silences the voice of God faster than blatant sin, or asking a question you already knew the answer to. Clearly he must've already known the answer to his question, because God hadn't said a word to him in reply. Realizing what he now needed to do, he picked up his things off the ground, and then started walking towards the driver. But, just as he did, he felt a strong voice in his heart tell him to wait. He wasn't sure if he should because, if they pulled away, he'd miss his chance to give them the key cards.

However, to his complete surprise, the driver started the car, pulled over to a nearby parking spot, and shut off the engine. An eyebrow went up slightly. Clearly that was why God had told him to wait. But the time to do so was over, and it was now time to act. He immediately scrambled into his truck, grabbed the two room keys he'd just picked up, and hurried over to the car. As he looked inside he noticed the driver praying. While he didn't want to interrupt them, he did see that they were in great need. So he knocked on the window causing them to jump in surprise. He watched as they quickly locked the doors and recoiled in fear. Given the situation, he could understand their feelings. The driver then lowered their window slightly, just enough to speak with him.

"Yes? Can I help you?" they asked.

"Are you Barton?" asked John.

The driver seemed surprised at this.

"Yeah," came the uncertain reply.

"You're heading east, right?"

"Yeah," replied the driver slowly.

John nervously fingered the two key cards in his hand.

"Well, last night God gave me a dream, and told me that you would be coming through here, and would need some place to stay for the night, and said to wait for you here. So here you are, and here I am, and...well, this is for you," he said awkwardly.

He then pressed the set of key cards through the window.

"These are the keys to the hotel room God told me to get for you. Um, I've arranged for dinner for you and your family and...well, um, God said He'd handle the rest."

He then gulped nervously, turned, headed over to his truck, and drove away. Yet, as awkward and embarrassed as he felt, he sensed an incredible peace flow over him, as though he'd not only done the right thing, but also something wonderful for the Lord. The only problem now was what to do about the two men who'd just robbed him. But that would be a problem that God would need to fix, which He would almost certainly do, and in the best, and most wonderful way possible.

Scene 2 - The Phone Call

"Hey, Rocket!"

A young teenage boy, with spiked orange, punk style hair, piercings all over his body, a multitude of tattoos, and a smart, snidely attitude, looked up from his school computer and stared across the desk at his best friend, a kid named Sidmond, or "Sid" for short, who was a nerd of the highest order, complete with glasses and a polka dot bowtie. Even though they were polar opposites in appearance, they both shared a common passion: Computers, and most especially hacking. Or "security evaluation and testing" as they preferred to call it. Rocket quietly studied his friend and grinned slyly.

"What's up, Sid?" he asked.

"Hey, are you up for something fun tonight?" asked Sid.

Rocket snorted.

"Dude, always. What'cha got in mind?"

"It's something one of my Facebook friends was talking about last night. He said his dad, back in the days before computers, did something called 'freaking.'"

Rocket screwed up his face in confusion.

"Like dressing up all weird and doing creepy things?"

Sid frowned.

"No, silly. It was phone hacking, but done in the age before computers. Basically, when you 'freaked' a phone call, you were hacking the phone system using analog methods. He even told me that there were people who were really good at it."

"Oh," said Rocket in interest. "Sounds like fun. But we can't do freaking anymore. Well, not that kind of freaking, anyways."

Sid laughed.

"Actually, we can. I've been doing a bunch of reading and, given that all the phones these days are digital, it'll be easy peazy for us."

Rocket perked up.

"Really," he said, his interest growing. "How easy are we talking? Easy, as in not getting caught and having the FBI kicking in our door, or easy as in calling someone and totally creeping them out."

Sid grinned.

"Both."

Rocket rubbed his hands together as a devilish grin drew across his face.

"Oooo, I'm game. When do we begin?"

"Log in to Mumble when you get home and we'll get started. I've got a tap in place in one of Level 3's regional Juniper routers we can use to freak some people."

Rocket looked at him in surprise.

"You've got a tap into a Juniper!? Dude, I'm jealous. How long have you had that!?"

"For about the last nine months," said Sid flatly.

"Man, you shouldn't be holding out on me like that! Imagine the fun we could've had with something so high up on the ladder of epic!" exclaimed Rocket.

"I didn't tell you because I know what you'd do, and I spent too much time breaking into it to risk you screwing it up for us," frowned Sid.

Rocket cringed at this.

"Oh, man, that's cold," he chuckled. "But you're probably right. So, you've had access to it all this time and they haven't found you yet?"

Sid shook his head.

"Not yet. But when they do their next IOS upgrade at the end of the month I'll lose the tap. So we may as well use it while it lasts."

"That's a drag, man. All that hard work wasted. But, um, how does a tap into a Level 3 regional router help us do some digital freaking?"

Sid grinned.

"It's one of the hubs Verizon routes through."

Rocket's eyes lit up.

"Oh.....my.....," he said with an amazed grin. "Dude, you serious!?"

Sid nodded.

"Dead serious."

Rocket let out a gleeful, almost devilish laugh. He was going to like this, and couldn't wait for the fun to start. Eventually the school day ended and Rocket wasted no time getting home. As soon as his feet hit the threshold of his front door he immediately shed everything from the school day, and then made a beeline for his bedroom, which was his own personal little man cave, and quickly began turning on all of his computer equipment. As soon as it was up he logged in, hoping to get online before Sid. However, much to his dismay, he didn't succeed, as Sid beat him online by a good two minutes.

Rocket put his headset on, and asked, "We live and ready?"

"I'm just waiting for my tools to load," replied Sid.

"Sweet! So who we pranking first? Got any names?"

"I was actually thinking about doing it randomly. If we start picking people we know it'll make it too easy for the Feds to figure out who we are. Pranking random people who don't know us will make it a lot harder for the Feds to point the finger at us."

"Yeah, good idea, man. I don't want no juvie time. Mom would ground me for a billion years if that happened, not to mention I'd lose all my gear," replied Rocket.

"I'd be more worried about the Feds locking us in a room and throwing away the room," quipped Sid.

Rocket rolled his eyes.

"Yeah, totally. That'd really be a bad day."

"Okay, my tools are loaded and I'm in. Looks like we'll only get three or four calls out of this before they drop the hammer on us. I'm seeing a monitor about two hops away keeping an eye on us. I'll try to route around it for right now and keep us alive as long as possible, but we could lose our link at any moment."

Rocket swore.

"I knew it was too good to be true!" he muttered.

"Don't panic, man. This just makes it more exciting."

"How so?"

"The thrill of the chase," chuckled Sid.

"If you say so," retorted Rocket.

Just then the sound of ringing briefly echoed in Rocket's ear.

"Wait! Are we calling someone already!?"

"Nope, just linking with Verizon. One second. Okay, we're in. Get your voice modulator ready. When you're up I'll put through a random call."

"Alright, modulator is up," replied Rocket.

He then chuckled slightly, his voice changing from clear and articulate to sounding like it'd been sent through a paper shredder.

"So who are we gonna pretend to be?" he continued.

A light, almost mischievous chuckle echoed from the other end.

"I say we go divine," replied Sid.

A devilish grin crossed Rocket's lips.

"Dude, god mode, bro," he replied.

"Alright, phone call going through," said Sid.

"Bring it on!"

The two boys then listened quietly as the sound of ringing could be heard in their headphones. This was soon followed by a click, and then someone answering.

"Hello?" came a voice across the line.

"Showtime," thought Rocket. "This is God," he said, his voice now big and booming as he adjusted his modulator to give his words a more authoritative feel.

"God!?" came the quivering reply.

"Yes, I am your creator!" bellowed Rocket, doing all in his power not to laugh.

"Oh, um, what...uh, what are you calling me for?" stuttered the caller.

"Wow, this is going better than I thought," typed Rocket in a separate chat window.

"Just stay on mission, or this prank will go south on us real fast," typed Sid in reply.

"Yeah, I'm on it," typed Rocket in return. "I want you to leave your house. *Now*!" he said aloud so that the caller could hear him.

"Leave it!?"

"YES, GO!" shouted Rocket, his voice booming over the phone. "Leave your home *now* and never look back! It is vital that you do this immediately and obey me without question!"

There was a pregnant, anxious pause on the other end. Sid and Rocket almost thought that the caller had hung up. Eventually there was the sound of a hard swallow that could barely be heard through their headphones.

"Alright, I'll go. But where?"

"Just go. I will show you the way."

"Yes, Lord," came the anxious reply.

The call then ended. The two boys laughed and whooped at this with glee.

"Oh man! That was tight! Dude, we need to do that again!" said Rocket.

"Can't. They cut the connection," replied Sid.

"Wait, what!?"

"Yeah, it looks like, despite my best efforts, they spotted us and cut the link. I guess we'll just have to try hacking something else so we can continue freaking."

Rocket grumbled.

"Great. And I was just starting to have fun."

"Don't worry. I got this. Give me about twenty minutes and I'll get us another tap. I just need to find someone who's still using the old IOS."

Rocket cocked an eyebrow.

"Are you sure there's anyone still out there? I mean, you did say that they were upgrading all the routers soon."

Sid laughed.

"Oh, plenty. They don't call them zero day exploits for nothing."

Rocket grinned devilishly.

"Cool, man, cool."

Scene 3 - The Instant Winner

Kelly, the store manager at a local gas station, walked into the building and headed straight towards his office in the back. He usually didn't come in this late in the afternoon as he preferred working during the mornings. But, because of a doctors appointment, and other previous commitments, he wasn't able to come to work today any sooner than this. As he walked into his office he was greeted by a pile of mail on his desk. He frowned slightly.

"There's never a day around here that I don't get buried in mail," he sighed.

As he picked up the thick stack of letters and flipped through them, one envelope in particular caught his attention. It was from corporate, and appeared urgent. Curious, he opened it and pulled out its contents. Inside was a packet filled with envelopes that contained prize slips, and gift certificates for a variety of local businesses, as well as several pages of instructions on what to do with them. As he was reading this his evening shift supervisor walked into the office.

"What's that? Something from corporate?" he asked.

Kelly pursed his lips slightly.

"Yeah. From what I'm reading they're having a contest, starting today of all days, and whoever wins gets one of these gift packs. The crazy part is, it's supposed to be a surprise, so they're not giving us any signage or a display of any kind to go with it. It's just random prizes to random customers."

The shift supervisor grunted.

"Gee, sure was nice of them to not notify us any sooner than this. It means I now have to sit down and plug all this stuff into the computer as quickly as possible before we get our butts chewed by corporate for not being on the ball with this," he muttered.

"Actually, you don't have to do anything. From what I'm reading, corporate has already done that for us, and sent us the necessary updates as part of our nightlies. So everything should already be live in system. Have you had any hits yet?"

"Not a single one, which I'm thankful for as I wouldn't have known what to do had we gotten a hit. So how does this notify us of a winner?"

"Well, from what I'm reading, whenever someone starts pumping, if they're a winner, it's supposed to trigger an alert in the store and immediately shut down their pump. We then give them the ticker tape parade, take a picture, give them their prize pack, and then send them on their way."

The shift supervisor chuckled.

"Why doesn't cool stuff like this ever happen to us?"

Kelly frowned.

"We're corporate slaves. They don't allow us to have good things like this. It'd make us think we were actually worth something," he quipped.

The supervisor laughed. Just then one of the tills in the store began chiming. A moment later an attendant came into the office with a befuddled look on their face.

"Sir, my terminal is doing something really weird. It's telling me to come get you because we have a winner?"

"And....we have our first victim," quipped the supervisor.

"That was timely," replied Kelly.

"First...eh, victim, sir?" asked the attendant.

Kelly waved dismissively.

"It's part of a surprise contest corporate is doing. I'll walk you through it in a minute as I've gotta put my credentials into the till in order to complete our side of the hoops and ladders necessary to make corporate happy. So did the alert give you a pump number?"

"Yes, sir. Pump nine. As soon as they tried fueling it completely shut them down. I told them to hold on while I figure out what's up," said the attendant.

"Alright, tell them to come on in. We'll explain things to them and then see to it that they get their prizes," said Kelly.

"Yes, sir."

The attendant then slipped away as Kelly gathered up the envelope full of prize slips and headed out to the counter where he found the attendant, and a surprised guest, waiting for him. He looked at the screen in front of him, plugged in his credentials, and was told which prize pack he was to give out. He fumbled through the envelope looking for the one the computer had specified, and soon found it. He then looked at the list of items on the envelope, and furrowed his brow slightly before looking up at the customer.

"Wow, are you the fortunate one today," he said.

"What do you mean?" asked the customer.

"Well, you're the first winner today in our surprise giveaway. And, according to this, not only do you get a free tank of gas, but you also get a hundred dollars cash, and a certificate for a free room and dinner at the Budget Inn just down the street."

The customer looked at him in shock!

"Dinner and a hotel room!?" they said in amazement.

"Yeah, as well as a hundred dollars of spending cash, and a tank of free gas."

He watched as the customer soon began to cry, and then hugged him with joy. Eventually they backed up apologetically, and smiled sheepishly. Kelly laughed.

"If only all of my customers were as grateful as you," he chuckled.

"Well, shall we get the picture?" asked the supervisor.

Kelly nodded, grabbed one hundred dollars out of the till, and then, with all of their prizes in hand, he posed with the customer, and the shift supervisor as they got their picture taken. Once they had done this, the customer went back outside and fueled their car before driving away, tears still streaming down their face. After seeing the customer's response to winning their prize, the supervisor felt good that they had gotten it, and not someone else.

"Ya know, there are some days that I actually love my job," he said.

Kelly laughed.

"Don't say that too loud or the oligarchs might hear you," he quipped.

The supervisor shrugged.

"Yeah, really. I mean, you can't go and let the minions be happy, now can you?"

Kelly shook his head.

"Not in this world, I'm afraid."

Scene 4 - The Late Run

Roger awoke with a start as his phone began ringing loudly. He then rubbed his eyes and rolled over to see who it was. He soon groaned when he saw the number. It was his employer, a local trucking company who specialized in urgent loads.

"Yeah," he said groggily as he answered the phone.

"Hey, Roger, sorry to do this to you on your day off, but can you come in? We've got a hot load due in Texas tomorrow morning and the driver who was scheduled to take it called in sick," came a voice on the other end.

Roger groaned.

"Come on, Chuck, you know I haven't had a day off in two weeks!! That's why I took today off, man."

"I know, and I understand, but we're short handed, and you're my only free driver right now. So I need your help, as I don't want to lose this contract by being late again."

Roger sighed.

"Alright, fine, I'll be there as soon as I can. When does this load have to be moving?"

"By 8:05 at the latest. I know that's really short notice, but do you think you can do it?"

Roger sighed again.

"Yeah, I can do it. I'll be there as fast as I can."

"Thanks, man, I appreciate it. And just for doing this I'll give you double pay for the load. Sound good?"

Roger laughed.

"Hey, for double pay I'll drive to the moon."

"Alright, then see you as soon as you get here."

Roger hung up, swore slightly, and then climbed out of bed as the sun started to break on the horizon as the first rays of day began peaking through the window. He quickly slipped on his clothes, and then trotted out to his truck. Twenty minutes later he pulled into work and parked near the loading docks. Not far away, Chuck, his boss, stood holding a clipboard and a set of keys.

"What'cha got for me today, chief?" he asked.

"You'll be driving rig twenty six twenty today. I know it's not your normal rig, but yours is in the shop for maintenance. So you get the backup rig," he said.

Roger shrugged.

"Hey, if it rolls, and doesn't chug, I don't care," he replied.

He then took the clipboard and keys, and made his way down the line of trailers as he headed out to pick up his truck, and grab his load. He then took a quick look at his watch. It was already 7:45am. He'd need to hurry if he wanted to be rolling by 8:05. He looked down at the clipboard and scanned the paperwork until he spotted the trailer ID.

"HB56905. HB. HB," he said to himself as he tried to spot the trailer he was looking for. Eventually he did. But, much to his chagrin, the trailer he was to haul that day had likely one of the most ridiculous paint jobs he'd ever seen. On the side of it was a gigantic pair of crocheted mittens laid out on a piece of butcher block. Below this were the words, "Go to Michigan. Don't Ask Why. Just Do It." He cocked an eyebrow slightly in disbelief.

"You see it too, eh?" said another driver nearby.

Roger turned around and looked at him.

"What's up with the weird trailer?" he asked.

"I don't know. It came in last night as an outbound hot load for this morning. Is that the one you're taking today?"

"Yeah. Gotta get it down to Texas by tomorrow morning, 9am."

"Wooowee! That *is* a hot load! You think you're gonna make it?"

"I don't know, but I'm gonna give it my best shot."

"Man, that's a long haul too. Got a backup driver going with you?"

"Nope, it's just me. Chuck is down a couple drivers, so I'm all he's got left."

The other driver looked at him in surprise.

"Man, that's rough."

Roger frowned.

"Yeah, tell me about it. Well, I've gotta get rolling."

"Alright, be careful out there and don't get caught speeding. That'll just make it worse."

Roger snorted.

"Yeah, tell me about it."

He then headed over to his truck, started it up, did his checks as fast as he could, and then backed up to the trailer. By the time he hooked, and was heading out of the lot, it was 8:09am. This trip was already starting out on a bad note, and he hoped it didn't get any worse. He then accelerated out of the yard and was soon on his way. But, as was typical for this part of town, it didn't take long before he became snarled in traffic, and his rig brought to an absolute and complete standstill. He then laid on his horn, but got no reaction from the other vehicles around him.

"Oh come on, people, MOVE! I've got a hot load here!" he shouted.

But, despite his best encouragements, the cars in front of him remained stationary. He honked again, but longer this time. Still nothing moved. It was a four wheel parking lot, and nobody was going anywhere. Eventually, the cars began to move again and, within a handful of minutes, he was able to reach the highway on ramp. It wasn't long after this that he was up to speed and rushing out of the city, already considerably far behind, hoping beyond hope in the back of his mind that he'd be able to make the delivery on time. That would mean going the entire distance without taking breaks of any kind, save for fuel. So he would need to use every trick in the book he knew if he wanted to get there in time. Even if he somehow came in late, the double pay for the load out, and the bobtail back, would be worth it. The only thing he had to do then was figure out where to get another day off. The way things were going it'd be next year before that happened.

Scene 5 - Stormy Weather

"Hey, Bert, come take a look at this," came a voice from the door.

A man sitting at the desk, the chief weatherman for KTLA TV, looked up to see one of his assistants standing there.

"Yeah, what is it, Sally?" he asked.

"Come have a look at this. You're not going to believe what just happened."

The man cocked an eyebrow at this, and then followed her out of the room, and over to a side office where a wall full of computers were chewing on data and displaying the expected results on a series of screens hanging on the wall.

Sally pointed at one of the screens, and said, "This is what I was talking about."

Bert walked up to the screen and had to adjust his glasses to be sure he wasn't seeing things.

"Where did that come from?" he asked.

"I don't know. The SPC just spotted it five minutes ago and gave us a ring to see if we'd seen it too."

"You mean the guys in Norman didn't see this coming?" he said in surprise.

"Apparently not. The guy I talked to said it caught them completely off guard."

Bert shook his head in disbelief.

"But we're in the dry season. This shouldn't be happening," he replied.

"I know. That's what *they* said. But apparently this spun up out of nowhere and is growing in intensity in ways they've never seen before. If it continues on its current path, it's going to spawn some really severe storms over LA. SPC is so spooked by this that they're considering issuing a tornado watch for our area."

Bert blinked and did a surprised double take.

"A tornado watch!? California doesn't get tornadoes! Well, not usually at least, and certainly never at this time of year!"

Sally shrugged.

"I agree. But how do you explain this?"

Bert looked at the screen again, and the prediction loop showing a rapidly escalating chance of severe weather over the city.

"Should we call a weather watch? Maybe warn people this is coming?" asked Sally.

Bert continued to study the screen in disbelief. He thought about this for a bit, and then shook his head.

"Not yet. Let's wait and see if SPC issues a watch first. If they do, we'll start warning people. Until then, we'll keep this quiet. No need to cry wolf and look like a fool."

Sally crossed her arms and snorted.

"If this goes in the direction that I think it will, crying wolf will be the least of our worries," she replied.

"Well then, let's grab the charts and make sure SPC is right, and that it's not another one of their computer glitches."

Sally watched as Bert stepped off the stage, away from the large green screen he used for weather reports, and over to where she was standing.

"Do you think anyone will pay attention to your report?" she asked.

Bert struggled to get the little clip-on mic off his lapel.

"I hope so. The problem is, I don't think they will. Tornadoes are a Midwest thing. We specialize in shake, rattle and roll, not twist and spin."

Sally laughed.

"They're both legitimate dance moves, ya know," she chided.

Bert smirked.

"Oh har har," he quipped.

Just then the shift producer sprinted into the room, a look of panic on her face.

"Get that mic back on! That storm just spawned a tornado!" she said.

"What!?" said Bert in surprise.

"Yeah, I just got a report from one of our field crews that a tornado is on the ground and completely gutting a couple suburbs in Chatsworth heading south towards US 101 and Topanga State Park."

Bert's head immediately snapped around to one of the monitors in the studio that showed the regional radar, and was aghast to see that the storm had not only rapidly intensified in the last few minutes, but was also showing a terrifying, classic tornado hook echo.

"Lord have mercy," he said.

Scene 6 - The Foreclosure

The senior loan manager for Shark's Loans, an unfortunately named mortgage lender that serviced the entire Los Angeles metroplex, looked up from his desk as one of his assistants leaned in the door.

"Sir, the Bakers are here to speak with you about their loan," said the assistant.

The manager groaned.

"Fine, I'll be right there," he muttered. He then shook his head, and said, "I don't know why they keep trying. Nothing they do will save that house."

"Should I tell them that, sir?"

The manager waved his hand dismissively.

"No, I need to tell them in person. Maybe then they'll finally get the message."

"Yes, sir," said the assistant as he turned and left.

Less than a minute later another employee came in and tossed a pile of folders on his desk. The manager looked at the employee curiously.

"What are these?" he asked.

"All the foreclosures for this week, twenty six in total. The courts just finished them up this morning. Every one of these properties is officially ours now."

The manager smiled and snorted gleefully.

"Finally. Anyone been evicted yet?"

"No, sir. We were waiting on the paperwork from the courts before we began."

"And do we have it now?" barked the loan manager.

"Yes, sir, we do."

"Well, then get on it, son! Get those houses cleared and on the market as fast as you can! I want my money!"

"Yes, sir."

As the employee left, the loan manager began flipping through the folders on his desk until he found one labeled "Baker". A devilish, evil grin crossed his face.

"There we go. Perhaps this will shut them up once and for all."

He quickly gathered up his paperwork and made his way out of the office, and over to the desk of one of his employees where a young couple sat with their two children as they waited anxiously for news about the fate of their home. The manager walked up to the desk, shooed the employee aside, and then sat down, a look of dark satisfaction growing in his eyes as the color drained from the faces of the distraught couple before him.

"Mr. and Mrs Baker," he began, his voice darkly gleeful.

"Tell us! Please! Do we still have the house?" sobbed the woman.

The already demonic grin on the manager's face seemed to grow even more evil.

"You do not," he said with dark satisfaction.

"But we can pay! Please! Just give us more time! I'm-" began the husband.

The manager immediately cut him off.

"Sir, I'm afraid to inform you, but your house has been foreclosed on. The agreement was that you would make *all* of your payments on time, and in their full amount, and if you couldn't, then the house would return to the possession of the bank. As it stands, you've failed repeatedly to pay your mortgage for the past six months. As such, per our agreement, your house now belongs to us."

A look of fear and trepidation washed over the faces of the young couple.

"But what will we do!? Where will we go!?" asked the husband.

The manager glared at them with cold, mute, uncaring eyes.

"To be honest, sir, I don't care. That's not my problem. Now, as this house has become a bank owned property, you have twenty four hours to vacate it, or we will come and remove you by force. And, if we do, you will be arrested and thrown in jail for trespassing, and your possessions taken to the dump, never to be seen again. Now leave this building, pack your things, and get off my land!"

The couple stared at the manager, devastated by what they'd just heard. Three years earlier, he and his associates had been so kind, accommodating, and willing to help them get into their first home. But now that they were no longer able to pay, it was an entirely different story, and they were entirely different people. The couple got up quietly, collected their children, and then made their way out of the building. The manager watched them go with devilish glee, and almost felt like cackling maniacally at their unfortunate plight. However, he wisely chose not to given that there were other potential customers in the bank that he didn't want to scare away. People had always told the Bakers that bankers were evil people. But never before had they seen such cruelty from a money lender. In many ways the rather unfortunate name of the bank, one "Shark's Loans", fit the institution ever so aptly, down to the very last speck of dust. But, just as the manager was about to get up and head to his office, another associate strolled up to him.

"Sir, I've got a lady here who wishes to speak with you about her mortgage. Apparently she's been foreclosed on too," said the employee.

"Do you have the file?" asked the manager flatly.

The employee held out a folder to the manager.

"Right here, sir," he said.

The manager grinned devilishly.

"Well then, I shall speak at length with her right now. It will give me the opportunity to ruthlessly crush the hopes and dreams of yet another now former client of ours."

The employee frowned slightly.

"You enjoy doing this, don't you?" he muttered.

"With every inch of my body," said the manager with demonic glee.

Just then one of his assistants came running in the door.

"Sir, the news is reporting that a tornado is leveling a large swath of Chatsworth!" he cried, fear echoing in his voice.

The manager looked at him in disbelief.

"A tornado!? That's preposterous! We don't get tornadoes out here!"

"Trust me, come look!" insisted the man.

The manager stood up, and then followed him over to a nearby lounge area where a number of customers, and all but two tellers, were huddled around the TV watching live coverage of an unfolding disaster in downtown Los Angeles. At first he couldn't figure out why everyone was so worked up about it. Those houses weren't his problem. But, just as he was about to leave, he caught sight of a street sign that looked all too familiar. He leaned forward and squinted carefully at the screen as he tried to get a better look. Just then the screen flashed to a map of the area being affected. The color immediately drained from his face as he realized the streets and cross streets that were being devastated by this storm. It was the same area that they'd just completed a sweeping series of foreclosures in. Now, much to his dismay, he was watching all that hard work turned to splinters.

"No, no, no, no, NO!" he cried as he ran for the back door.

"Where are you going?" asked one of the assistants.

But the manager said nothing. He merely jumped into his car and raced across town to where the tornado was ravaging neighborhood after neighborhood like a gigantic, windy brushhog of doom. Eventually the storm dissipated, leaving the skies over the city once again clear and sunny. Upon seeing this, and wanting to know if all was well or, at the very least, how bad the damage was, the loan manager continued to drive with great haste, and fear, towards the neighborhoods that his bank now owned. Eventually he arrived at the edge of the first neighborhood and was greeted by a scene of unbelievable, biblical level carnage and absolute destruction. Every single house that the bank now owned in that neighborhood was gone;

completely wiped from existence, with only the foundation slabs remaining. However, to his complete surprise and astonishment, as though defying all possible reason and logic, every house within those neighborhoods that the bank didn't own still remained, completely untouched, and without so much as even a single blade of grass being out of place anywhere on their properties. As the loan manager looked on at this in abject confusion and disbelief, a local police officer walked up next to him.

"Got a home in there, buddy?" he asked.

The manager turned and looked at the cop in confusion for a moment before regaining his composure, albeit barely.

"I work for Shark's Loans and we own this neighborhood. All those houses are...well, *were* ours," he said, his voice cracking.

The officer shook his head.

"Oh really? Darned shame if you ask me," he replied.

Just then something struck him.

"Wait, did you say Shark's Loans?"

"Yeah, that's the company I work for. I'm the senior loan manager."

A knowing, almost devious grin grew across the officer's face.

"Is that so? Well, then I guess you won't be screwing over anyone else anymore. Not after the losses you'll take from this. Oh, and by the way. Just so you know, since these properties are now yours, you're responsible for cleaning up this mess. Now get to work before I start fining you for littering."

The manager looked at the officer in shock.

"How am I responsible for this!?" he screamed.

"Your property, your problem. Now get cleaning."

The manager growled slightly.

"This is *so* not my day," he moaned.

Scene 7 - The Golden Ticket

Gert, a wealthy old businessman of nearly sixty years, strolled slowly out of the grocery store, and across the parking lot towards his SUV. It wasn't a big grocery store, and was actually kinda small by modern standards. But, then again, so was the town. In fact, it was surprisingly small for a city so close to Omaha, and not that far north of Interstate 80. Even so, it was a quaint little town, with some big city benefits, but a small town feel. As he crossed the parking lot the nearby street lights flickered on as evening began to settle in over the little city. It wouldn't be but another twenty minutes before the sun would set for the day. To make matters worse, if he didn't hurry up, he'd be late for his meeting with two potentially new and lucrative clients.

He soon reached the driver's side door of his SUV and set his bags on the ground. Even though the Super Saver, a local discount grocery, was more or less a poor man's store, he still loved to shop there. Especially for the prices. Just because he was rich didn't mean he was against saving a buck or two whenever he could. As he pulled his keys out of his pocket, a hint of green on his front windshield caught his eye. He paused for a moment and leaned to his left just enough to see what it was. There, much to his surprise, was a brand new, crisp, uncirculated one hundred dollar bill. The sharp and savvy old man cocked an eyebrow slightly and then slowly slid his keys back into his pocket as his head began a slow, careful scan of the parking lot around him.

He'd heard about things like this before. In fact, one of his friends up in Lincoln had fallen prey to it once before, causing him to lose a brand new SUV to a couple of big city thugs who'd pulled the same scam. The trick was simple. Place a hundred dollar bill in the wiper of the victim's car, and when they got out to take it from the windshield, one of the thieves would race up and make off with the car. Gert wasn't about to let that happen to him. He continued to scan the parking lot carefully, half expecting to see armed thugs storming towards him at any moment ready to beat him within an inch of his life in order to steal his SUV and sell it on the black market.

But, to his surprise, he didn't see anyone moving. Even so, as his one hand was firmly securing his keys in his pocket again, his other was pulling his cell phone out of his suit pocket. A few pecks later he'd dialed 911. He wasn't about to become a victim, nor let anyone else be one either. Just then his eyes, still sharp and clear despite his advanced age, caught sight of an older model Pontiac sitting one row over, and several cars down from him. Two young men, one Latino, and the other dark skinned, glared back at him. Apparently they weren't too fond of the idea that he'd caught onto them. Even worse, he was now on the phone, likely calling the police.

"911, what's your emergency?" came a voice in his ear.

"Yes, my name is Gert. I'm down here at the Super Saver on 2nd street and I've got a couple thugs in a late model green Pontiac trying to do a car jacking on me," he replied.

The operator seemed a bit surprised at this.

"Are they physically threatening you or trying to assault you, sir?"

"No, but they're eyeing my Escalade like a slab of meat. They left a crisp hundred on my windshield in an attempt to steal my car, and don't seem all that pleased that I caught onto their scheme," he replied.

He then smiled and waved at the two men who, in turn, flipped him off, started their car, and began to drive away. As they did, Gert read off their plate to the operator.

"Yeah, they're just starting to leave, although they don't seem to be in a big hurry. They might be waiting for an opportunity to strike someone else," he continued.

"Alright, sir. We'll handle this. If you're not already in your vehicle, please get inside, lock your doors and wait for further instructions," said the operator.

"Nah, I don't think they're a threat to me anymore, but you'll want to bag them before they can go and hit someone else."

"Alright, sir. But please stay in the area so that, if the officers need help identifying the vehicle, they can ask you for information."

"I wish I could, but I've got a meeting I need to get to. If they have any questions, you've got my number. Just ring me up and I'll gladly help out."

"Alright then, sir, be safe."

Gert closed his phone and stuck it in his pocket. He then eyed the crisp hundred dollar bill pinned under his wiper blade and wondered what to do with it. Given his vast fortune it wasn't like he needed another one of those in his wallet. For him, something like that was pocket change. Yet he didn't want to just randomly leave it behind. His eyes soon caught sight of an older model car, one that had definitely seen better days, parked in front of him. Immediately an idea struck him. While he didn't need the extra money, the owner of that car almost certainly did. So he reached into his wallet, took out two more crisp hundred dollar bills, and added them to the one that was on his windshield. He quickly clipped them under the wiper of the other car, climbed into his SUV, and then drove off. No more than a block away Gert passed a group of three police cars, and the late model Pontiac he'd seen earlier. He then spotted two men splayed across its hood in handcuffs being read their rights. He chuckled lightly to himself.

"Crime doesn't pay, does it, boys?"

He then headed down the street to his meeting hoping that, whoever got the money he'd left behind, would put it to good use. Just then he smacked himself on the forehead in an expression of self chastisement.

"Augh! And then I went and forgot the mustard again!"

Scene 8 - Built Like A Tank

Benny, a long time police veteran, was out on the local interstate doing his normal afternoon patrols when he spotted something unusual happening with the vehicle in front of him. It wasn't the fact that it'd clearly seen far too many hours on the road. But rather, it was the way the driver's side rear wheel was wobbling back and forth as though it was ready to come off. Wanting to intervene before anything bad happened, he lit up the car, his lights and siren screaming as he signaled for the driver to pull over. But, before either car knew what'd happened, the left rear wheel well disintegrated, sending the tire, metal bits, sparks and a whole shower of other things spraying all over the road. Benny instinctively swerved to miss the cloud of debris that exploded from the vehicle as it slowly came apart in front of him. Moments later it skid wildly across the road and into the center median.

It soon collided head on with a guard rail which ripped the bottom out of the car, and sent it flying high into the air. Benny's heart nearly leapt out of his chest as he watched what he thought would almost certainly be a fatal accident unfolding in front of him. But, much to his relief and surprise, the vehicle, or what was left of it, landed in the upright position and soon came to a full stop. It was badly mangled and shredded, but still somehow intact. Well, mostly. If there was one thing he had to admit he liked about the older cars was that they were built like tanks, and could take a beating. And this one was no exception. He then immediately pulled to the side of the road and got on the radio to home base.

"Dispatch, this is 405, I've got a 10-51 at mile marker 233 eastbound. Need a wrecker, ambulance and fire immediately. Possible multiple casualties."

"Roger, 405. Dispatching resources immediately," came the reply.

Benny then carefully pulled out into the debris strewn highway, placing his car into the path of oncoming traffic to prevent anyone else from passing through until he'd had a chance to deal with the accident, and cleanup the mess it'd left behind. He then got out of his cruiser and hurried over to where the car now dangled awkwardly on the shattered guard rail, expecting to find the worst when he arrived. But, as he approached the driver's side of the car he found a woman, and her two children, standing there in the highway median, staring at the wreck in surprise and confusion. This made his blood boil. The accident wasn't even a minute old and rubberneckers were already on the scene gawking like "a bunch of over stuffed monkeys" as he liked to say.

"Excuse me, ma'am, but you'll have to step back! I need to get to the passengers in this vehicle," he barked.

"Um, we *are* the passengers. That's our car," said the woman.

The officer looked at them for a moment like they were nuts, and then shooed them to the side as he made his way over to the driver's side front and rear doors which he found, much to his surprise, open and the occupants gone. He then turned and looked at the woman and her two kids, then the vehicle, the woman, and finally the vehicle. He scratched his head in utter amazement and disbelief.

He then pointed a thumb at the vehicle, and asked, "This is *your* car!?"

"Yes, officer. That's ours. Or what's left of it," nodded the woman, who was unharmed, but clearly in shock.

Benny tilted his head back slightly and scratched his head. By all rights, given the condition of the vehicle, they should've had at least a few cuts and bruises. Yet there they stood without so much as a scratch on them.

"Are you alright, ma'am?" he asked after a few moments.

"We're fine," she replied.

Just then the echo of sirens could be heard in the distance.

"Alright, stay right there, ma'am. I want the ambulance to check you out before we do anything else."

The woman nodded. About a minute later a fire truck, an ambulance, and two more patrol cars pulled up to the accident, they too expecting the worst, and immediately headed over to the vehicle to deal with what they knew would almost certainly be a messy situation. They even shooed the woman and her kids away just like Officer Benny had, thinking they were just nosy rubberneckers. And, in the same way as Officer Benny, they too were shocked to learn that they were the passengers of the car, and were miraculously, and completely unharmed.

"But...but, how!? Nobody should've walked away from that in one piece!" protested one of the firemen.

"Divine intervention. It's the only explanation," said another.

"Wow, talk about guardian angels working overtime," said yet another fireman.

"Alright, ma'am," said one of the officers. "Come over here and we'll get you checked out. I wanna be completely sure you're alright."

The woman and her two children followed him over to the ambulance while the second officer walked up to the car and inspected it. He shook his head.

"The only thing that saved their bacon was that this car is a tank! Given the damage that it took, this could've ended a lot worse than it did," said the officer.

Benny nodded.

"Yeah, but I think I'm gonna agree more with that firefighter. This was God in every measure of the word. There's no way she could've walked away from this had it not been for Him protecting her."

The other cop snorted.

"Believe your religious nonsense all you want. I say she lucked out."

Benny looked back at the woman briefly, and the happy looks on the faces of the paramedics, and then back at the other officer.

"Not me. This was absolutely a God thing," he said.

He then walked over to the woman and checked on her.

"What's the prognosis?" he asked.

"There's not a blessed thing wrong with any of them, officer. Not even a bruise," said one of the paramedics.

"That's good to hear," replied Benny.

"But what do I do now? I'm thankful we survived. But now I have no car, and no way to get where we're going," said the woman.

"Where you headed to?"

"Michigan."

"Where in Michigan?" he asked.

The woman shrugged.

"God hasn't told me yet."

Benny cocked an eyebrow at this, but didn't argue the point. Especially after what he'd just seen.

"Alright, tell ya what. I'm not sure what I can do for you on that part, but we'll at least get you into town, and then we'll let the garage decide what needs to happen from there. Hopefully they can get you on your way again."

The woman nodded.

"Okay. Thank you," she replied.

Scene 9 - The Sleeper

Davis, one of the mechanics for the local auto garage, looked up as a tow truck pulled into his parking lot dragging the saddest looking car he'd seen in ages.

"Hey, Gerd, come check this out," he said.

An older man came out of the back, wiping grease off his fingers with an already well soiled shop towel, and nearly did a doubletake when he saw it. Badly damaged cars came through his garage on a regular basis every month, but this one took the cake.

"Wow, who's wonder wreck is that?' he asked.

Davis pointed at the passengers in the cab of the tow truck.

"Those three."

"Are we actually gonna have to fix that piece of junk?" muttered Gerd.

Davis shook his head.

"They look like a hard luck case to me. So probably not. This car will likely just end up as a write-off."

Gerd frowned.

"Great. In other words, we can forget this job," he muttered.

"Probably."

Gerd rolled his eyes, turned and headed back into the shop as Davis approached the tow truck driver.

"So, what'cha got?" he asked.

"Well, according to the cops, this lady was driving down the interstate when the car pretty much blew up under her. Debris everywhere. Somehow she came out of it with no problems, and merely coasted to a spectacular finish in the median with what was left of it. He said he's seen a lot, but that one took the cake," said the driver.

Davis looked at the car again. The tow truck driver's story was starting to explain the odd condition of the vehicle.

"Alright, just drop it off over there and we'll have a look at it," he said.

"Will do, boss."

The driver then carefully backed his truck around, eased expertly into a parking spot, slid the car off the tow bed, talked with the car owner briefly, and then headed on down the road. As the tow truck driver drove away, Davis stepped over to the vehicle and began inspecting it. What he saw was not good, and it just got worse as he went. After a bit he looked up to see the woman standing next to him looking anxiously at her car.

"Can it be fixed?" she asked apprehensively.

"Well, I hate to say it, but no. It's bad enough that you pretty much dropped the entire rear end on the ground. But, to make matters worse, you also snapped the frame, probably when you made that spectacular nose dive into the median that the tow driver told me about. I'm actually surprised you walked away from that alive, to be honest. Either way, she's not going anywhere ever again. She's as cooked a goose as you're gonna get."

A look of dejected sadness grew across the woman's face.

"So it's a total loss?" she asked.

"I'm afraid so, ma'am," said Davis.

Her complexion then became even more disappointed and sad, as if that was even possible at this point. Davis felt bad for the woman, realizing that she probably had little if any money to her name, and now didn't have a car either. He shook his head at this, as he wished he could do something for her. But, unfortunately, there was nothing that could be done. At least, not without spending a fortune that she clearly didn't have. But, just then, as he was beginning to walk away, something caught his eye. He paused for a moment, and soon turned back to the car, not wanting to believe what he was seeing. Eventually he reached over and gently pried open the mangled hood. What he found underneath made his eyes grow three sizes bigger.

"Gerd! Get out here!" he shouted.

The older mechanic came trotting out to the car.

"Yeah, what's....whoa," he said upon seeing what Davis was looking at. "Is that..." he began, still in utter shock.

"I think it is, which means we're looking at the sleeper of the century," said Davis.

"Sleeper?" asked the woman curiously.

"Yeah, in automotive terms a 'sleeper' is a car that looks normal on the outside, but has some serious muscle under the hood. What makes yours a sleeper is this engine. It's a 1973 Oldsmobile model W-43, 455ci Experimental, which is one of the most sought after, and rarest muscle car engines out there."

The woman looked at him in confusion.

"Okaaaaaay, but what does that do for me?" she asked.

"Lady, you're sitting on a gold mine. In fact, tell ya what. I'll make you a deal. $500 and I'll take the car off your hands no questions asked."

The woman paused, as though his offer was beyond ridiculous, which it was. Seeing this, and fearing that she might bolt, and take the engine with her, as well as a potential windfall profit, Gerd grabbed Davis by the arm.

"One second, ma'am," he said apologetically.

He then dragged Davis to the other side of the small parking lot, and began to glare at him angrily. Clearly he was not happy with the younger man.

"Davis! $500!? Really!?" he said angrily through gritted teeth.

"What? It's a monster in a wreck. I'm sure that's all she'd expect to get out of it."

"You idiot! That engine, even as it sits now, is worth almost twenty grand!! If we do some upgrades and rebuild it, we could get almost forty grand out of that thing! And you want to quote her five hundred!? Are you freaking nuts!? If you bid her that low she'll take it somewhere else and we'll lose that money!"

Davis snorted.

"She's just a dumb broad. What's she know about engines?"

"Did you see the look on her face, and the way she hesitated!? She knows way more than she's letting on. I say we give her five grand."

"Five grand!? That's way too much! Besides, in her current condition she'll gladly take the five hundred and leave."

Gerd growled at Davis and stuck his finger in his chest.

"Davis, don't screw this up for us! We stand to make a mint off this. If you're not gonna give her the money for it, then I will!"

Davis looked at the older mechanic and narrowed his eyes slightly. He didn't like the idea of sinking so much cash into any project up front, despite what they could make from this purchase. And yet, if he didn't, he stood to lose a large and tidy profit if Gerd, or someone else bought it out from under him. He sighed.

"Alright, I'll do it. But you're splitting the bill with me."

Gerd snorted.

"Given what we'll make from it, I have no problem with that."

The two men then walked back to the woman, who now looked even more perplexed than before, and smiled.

"Tell you what. My partner and I have been discussing this, and we realize that you drive a hard bargain. So we're willing to give you a thousand," said Davis.

"Davis," hissed Gerd.

But the woman didn't appear willing to budge. However, it wasn't because she was holding out for the best price. She honestly had no idea what was going on.

"$1500?" asked Gerd.

"Two grand," retorted Davis.

"Three grand."

"Alright, five grand, and not a dime more," snapped Davis.

The woman looked back and forth between the two men, completely uncertain what was happening, and not sure what to say.

Believing that she was still holding out for the best price, and knowing that Davis wasn't willing to make the investment, Gerd decided to take the dive and risk it all himself.

"Ma'am, since my partner here won't offer you a fair price for that engine, I'll give you $7500 out the door. Deal?" he asked.

The woman appeared to think this over for a bit, and then nodded.

"Okay, I can do that," she said hesitantly. "But what do I do about a car? I obviously can't drive this one anymore."

The two men looked at each other briefly before retreating across the parking lot again.

"She's got a point. What's she going to do for a car? I mean, yeah, she'll get $7500 from us. But then she's still stranded," said Gerd.

Davis, realizing that he was gonna be losing out on this engine if he didn't do something quick, came up with an idea.

"I've got a buddy of mine down at Kent's Auto that owes me a favor. A *BIG* favor. Why don't we talk with him and see if he can't get her a car, and maybe some gas money for that seventy five hundred we're gonna give her," he said.

Gerd pondered this briefly.

"Well, I'm okay with that. But if your buddy can't get her a new car with that $7500 out the door, then we're gonna need to cover the difference," he replied.

"What!?" yelped Davis.

"Remember, that engine isn't ours yet. Until she's satisfied with this deal, we're still standing here with our butts in the wind. So we've gotta make her happy, even if it hurts us a little. Trust me, it'll be worth it," said Gerd.

Davis pondered this for a moment before glancing at the woman who still looked just as confused as before. He eventually sighed.

"Fine. Let's get her taken care of so we can get that engine," he grumbled.

Gert smiled at this.

"Good choice, son," he replied.

The two men then returned to the woman with smiles on their faces. As best she could tell, they had come to a decision that they both liked. She just hoped it would be one that she liked too.

"Ma'am, we've talked it over, and come to a decision about your car. You obviously need a new vehicle, and we need that engine. So here's what we're gonna do. I have a buddy of mine down at the local dealership who owes me a favor. So I'm going to talk to him about getting you a good used car, and everything you need for it, and we'll pay for it in exchange for your engine. That way you'll have the new car that you need, and we'll get your engine in return. Sound like a deal?" said Davis.

The woman smiled happily at this.

"I'll take it."

Part 2 – The Play

Jenna was a simple girl with simple needs. Born and raised in Los Angeles, her life had been filled with everything she thought she'd ever need: A good husband, a good house, a good job, a great car, lots and lots of cash in the bank, and so much more. But two years earlier that perfect life had come crashing down around her. With the sudden death of her husband, and the simultaneous economic implosion of 2008, all of that had gone up in smoke. Even her sizable savings and investments had been reduced to a tiny fraction of their original value in only a few hours. To make matters worse, she'd been forced to use what little remained to bury her husband, leaving her with literally nothing to her name. In a strange twist of fate, similar tragedies had also befallen everyone else in her neighborhood at the same time, forcing all of them to pack up and leave their once luxurious homes one by one until only Jenna remained.

But that was just the first of many repeated insults to hit her and her family. In order to put food on the table, and keep the lights on, they'd been forced to sell off everything they owned. She'd even had to trade in her expensive luxury car for an old beater that'd already seen far too many miles, and too many years on the road. But even that only helped for a little while as she eventually ran out of things to sell, leaving her with empty shelves, an empty bank account, and two hungry mouths to feed. It soon reached a point where all they had left was two changes of clothes each, and a handful of blankets on which they slept. There was nothing else, as even the house had been repossessed. The only reason they weren't out on the street already is because the bank hadn't thrown them out yet.

But that was coming soon enough. As Jenna sat alone in a corner of the empty living room, waiting for her kids to return home from school, she quietly read words of comfort from the Psalms, and prayed to God that He would take care of her and her children in this most desperate time of need. It made her think of a time, not two years earlier, when she wouldn't even glance sideways at a bible, let alone read it. And yet now, after her world had so painfully imploded around her, she'd found a peace and security in God's word unlike at any time before in her life. It was during her time of grieving, not long after laying her husband to rest, that a couple from a local church had invited her and her two kids to dinner one night. They'd help console the grieving family and, in the process, led them all to a saving knowledge of Jesus Christ.

In the days following that dinner, God had called the couple away to other locations halfway around the world to do much the same thing as they'd done with her: Namely leading others to the Lord. As such they'd left Jenna and her two kids in the capable hands of their local church. And it'd been that body of believers that'd sustained them through the many hard times that followed. But it was also those same hard times that'd eventually forced that church to close its doors. And it wasn't as if something bad had happened to the people. Instead, it was because so few church members still remained in the area due to job losses, financial struggles, relocation by their employers, or other things. Because of this they'd chosen to take what few of their members remained and merge them with another congregation across town. That, in turn, had left Jenna in a lurch.

Where once her church was within walking distance, a blessing for someone with very little money, it was now much too far away to be visited regularly on her meager finances. It was thoughts like these that pricked at the edge of her mind as she dutifully tried to read her bible. Just then she heard the mail truck pull up outside. It had to be an odd thing for the mail carrier to have to drive through this area of back to back foreclosed homes to deliver mail to the only remaining occupied dwelling in the entire area. The experience for them had to be surreal. The thought that her house would soon join the others as well was enough to make her cry. She struggled hard to fight back the tears.

When would these trials end? When would the hits stop coming? She knew Jesus was with her, even now, and watching over her day by day. But that didn't make the battle any easier. Finally, deciding that the best thing for her to do right now would be to see what'd arrived, she got up and walked outside to her mailbox hoping beyond hope for a miracle. As she anxiously opened the box she found two letters inside, one from the state welfare office, and the other from Shark's Loans, the servicer of her mortgage. She carefully opened the one from the welfare office, hoping deep in her heart that it would be good news, only to have those hopes crushed by learning that she'd again been rejected for public aid. She now found herself with nowhere else to turn.

Her church still helped her out periodically with food, or a bit of money to pay bills, but even that aid was running out, not because they didn't want to help her, but because they couldn't anymore. Distance, and an overwhelming demand from their community, had emptied their food banks and resources so severely that what little remained was carefully rationed out. She sighed again and then opened the letter from Shark's Loans. If the rejection from the state hadn't been bad enough, the news in the second letter was worse. Despite spending time earlier in the week pleading with the loan agent for more time to get back on her feet and to let her keep her house, Shark's had completed final foreclosure and was now demanding that she be out by the end of the month.

A tear streamed down her face as she thought about the meeting. She'd come into the office alone, apprehensive about talking with them, but hoping for some kind of human charity. Unfortunately, her meeting, which had taken a grand total of five minutes, had ended in the worst possible way. She had been told that, if she didn't come up with the entire amount she owed, by the end of the week, she would lose her house. She'd hoped that getting approved for welfare might help her make at least one of those back payments. But with that hope gone, she knew for certain that they would end up in a homeless shelter, or worse yet, on the streets themselves. The tears, which had only been a trickling stream before, now became a gushing, unbridled fountain of pain.

"Why, God, why!? Why are You doing this to us!?" she cried. "I thought You loved me and my children!"

As strange as it still was to her, she felt a peace that passes all understanding flow over her as if to say, "But I do."

"Then why are you taking everything away from us!? If You love us, why won't You help us save our house!? WHY!?!?" she cried.

But, to that question, there was no answer. Just then she felt the winds pick up slightly. She looked up at the sky and, through her tears, was surprised to see dark storm clouds gathering on the horizon. This time of year was usually marked by severe drought and lots of clear, sunny days. To see clouds of any kind was a rare event. Just then the school bus turned down her street. Not wanting her kids to see her this way, she hurried inside and closed the door. She then watched from the living room window as the bus pulled to a stop in front of the house, dropped off her two children, a young boy of ten, and a little girl seven years of age, and then pulled away. She sighed again and then took the two letters in her hand and slid them into her backpack that leaned against the living room wall. She didn't want the children to see them and know what was coming. The two children came in the front door a moment later happy and giggling from the school day, despite knowing that they would come home to an empty house that would soon no longer be theirs.

"How was your day?" asked Jenna, doing her best to hide her tears.

Brad, Jenna's son, gave his mother a beaming smile and then expounded to her a whole list of exciting things that'd happened that day, including a surprise field trip to the zoo. Emma, her daughter, wasn't far behind with her tales of adventure and excitement at school that day. Despite all they'd lost, all the hardship they faced, and the bleak future that stood before them, there was still an innocent joy about them. She could only attribute that to their faith in God. If Jesus hadn't been the center of their lives, she didn't know what kind of a mess her children would be in. This, in itself, helped her to feel a little better. If her children could find joy, even in a dark situation like this, then so could she!

She immediately set about fixing them a dinner of peanut butter sandwiches, the very last of the food in the house, and then sent them to do their homework while she went about the last few chores she was still able to do. One of those was packing the car in preparation for leaving the house once and for all, and never coming back. Even though there wasn't much to pack, she was going to ensure that they brought with them all they had left, whatever little that was. Just then, much to her surprise, her phone rang. What made it even stranger was that it hadn't been on all week as she'd been saving the battery for emergency calls only. Especially since the power had been turned off, leaving her with no way to charge it once the battery ran down. She also didn't have active cell service anymore. Yet, there it was, ringing. So the call was surprising to her. Who could be calling her? And, for that matter, how was it even on!? It'd been off only moments earlier. She cautiously picked up her phone, and saw that the caller was listed as anonymous. She wasn't sure she wanted to answer it, but felt a gentle coaxing to do so.

"Hello?" she answered.

A deep, authoritative voice boomed from the other end.

"This is God," it said.

Jenna's heart nearly leapt out of her chest.

"God?" she replied in a quavering voice.

"Yes, I am your creator!" bellowed the voice.

"Oh, um, what...uh, what are you calling me for?" she stuttered, nervous at the prospect of being called by the Almighty.

She was also slightly surprised that this was even happening, given that God had never contacted her like this before. At least, not that she could remember.

"I want you to leave your house. *Now!*" boomed the voice on the other end.

Jenna blinked slightly. Was God getting into the eviction business too!?

"Leave it!?" she asked in surprise.

"YES, GO!" boomed the voice. "Leave your home *now* and never look back! It is vital that you do this immediately, and obey me without question!"

Jenna was shocked. To begin with she'd never actually spoken verbally with God, and secondly she'd never expected Him to speak with her this way on their first audible interaction. Even so, she didn't want to disobey Him.

"Alright, I'll go. But where?" she asked.

"Just go. I will show you on the way."

"Yes, Lord," she replied anxiously, and immediately hung up.

She then stood there for several moments in stunned silence, oblivious to the still darkening skies, and increasingly stronger winds outside. Thunder then boomed in the distance as she tried to get her mind around what'd just happened. Then, must to her surprise, a still small voice tugged at her heart.

"Go," it said.

Suddenly Jenna snapped back to reality, quickly shaking off the shock of the moment and refocusing her thoughts to the here and now.

"Brad, Emma, grab everything you have and get in the car!" she said as she turned and hurriedly began packing up the last of their possessions.

"Why? Are we going somewhere?" asked Brad.

"Just pack your things and get in the car, now!" came the sharp reply.

The two children looked at each other briefly, and then, scooping up their homework and school bags, did as their mom asked, and made a beeline for the car, their arms full to overflowing as Jenna worked quickly to stuff their last few things in the trunk. She then started the car and backed out just as a strong gust of wind shook the house like a hammer. It was at this moment that she looked up and caught sight of a terror she'd not seen since the summer she'd spent with her aunt in the Midwest as a child. It was a gigantic, raging tornado, and it was bearing down on their house!

"Mama, what is that?" asked Emma.

But Jenna didn't waste time explaining. She punched the gas, causing the car's tires to squeal and smoke as it raced down the short driveway, and out into the street with a roar! She then slammed it into drive and bolted down the street as debris of every shape and size began raining down around her. She did her best to keep the car under control, despite the raging winds, while at the same time keeping an eye on the twister as it gained ground behind them. By now her kids, having figured out what was happening, were screaming in panic.

"Lord, help us, help us, help us, help us!" she said, repeating this over and over again as her heart raced in fear.

The tornado soon turned down her street and began obliterating every single house that was there like they were made of match sticks. Eventually, though, the tornado abated, first stopping in its tracks, and then roping out before ascending back into the sky. Seeing this Jenna gave a nervous sigh of relief. Yet, at the same time, there was a tug of loss in her heart. Not only had they lost the house legally, but it was now completely destroyed as well. They now truly had nowhere to go anymore. Once again the tears became a river down Jenna's face as she came to the end of their street, and then did her level best to merge into traffic on the main road without hitting anyone. But, try as she might, she could barely see through the tears, which nearly caused her to wreck several times. So, rather than risk killing herself and her children, she pulled off the road and into a nearby gas station. She soon found a parking space facing the street and shut off the car.

"Are we alright?" asked Emma, fear still in her voice.

However, Jenna didn't respond as she was too busy trying to regain her composure. Just then, much to her surprise, Brad leaned forward and put his hand on her shoulder.

"Mama, you always taught us that, when things are scary, to call on Jesus," he said.

This brought a smile to Jenna's face. Despite all of the excitement and insanity they'd just gone through, her son still held strongly to his faith.

"Out of the mouths of babes," she thought.

She then lowered her head and began to pray, her two children joining her as she did.

"Dear Lord, thank You for sparing our lives, and saving us from that disaster, to which I have no explanation for its appearance, or why You allowed it to happen. But Lord, You know our needs. You know we now have no roof over our heads, and no place to call home. Where do we go, Lord, and what do we do? We have nothing, except You. What is Your will for us, and where do we go?"

Just then they were all startled by the loud blast of a truck horn. Jenna quickly shook it off and tried to concentrate on her prayers again, struggling desperately to hear from God, and to learn what it was He wanted them to do. But, as she did, the horn blew again, this time much louder and longer. It was shortly after this that she heard her daughter gasp and then giggle in glee.

"Mama, look! Jesus is talking to us!" said Emma.

Jenna looked up in curiosity to see what her daughter was talking about and soon spotted a most peculiar sight. There, stopped on the street in front of them, was an eighteen wheeler that was hauling a trailer on which was painted two crocheted mittens laid out on a piece of butcher block. But it wasn't the mittens that interested her. It was the words that were written at the bottom of the picture.

"Go to Michigan. Don't ask why. Just do it."

Jenna blinked. She'd heard of God talking to people in odd ways, but never like this. Was Michigan really where God wanted them to go? That was halfway across the country! But no more than had she thought this than she felt a gentle nudge in her spirit.

"Go."

She looked down at her gas gauge. Less than a quarter of a tank.

"But I don't have enough money or gas to make it, and that's a long ways away, Lord," she quietly prayed.

"Go," repeated the voice with a kindly smile.

Jenna gave a nervous sigh. This was going to be a massive leap of faith for her. But, if that's what God wanted, then that's what she'd do. Now all she had to do was get out into traffic, which currently resembled a massive parking lot. But, just as this thought crossed her mind, the traffic suddenly cleared. She then started the car, and began to drive. Wherever it was that God was taking her, and her children, would be, beyond a shadow of a doubt, the greatest leap of faith she had ever experienced. And, while she wasn't quite sure how she'd get all the way to Michigan as she'd been asked to do, she knew that if they could at least get out of LA, then they could figure out the rest from there. Or, more precisely, God would. They just had to follow directions, whatever that might be.

Jenna looked down at her gas gauge and didn't like what she was seeing. The old car was eating gas much faster than she'd expected, and the needle was already getting far too cozy with the big red E on the wrong end of the dial. She looked up in the rear view mirror and saw that her two children, much to her relief, were now sound asleep. The stress of the day had apparently caught up with them and they'd decided to power nap in the back seat while mom took them to wherever God was leading. Not sure what she would do next, especially given how late it was, she pulled off the highway and headed for the first gas station she could find. But it was closed for repairs. So she tried pulling into several others, but was again blocked, despite her best efforts. Eventually she was able to find an open station that she could pull into and soon made her way to a pump. She then stopped and turned off the car, lowered her head, and began to pray.

"Lord, You know our situation. You've told us to go all the way to Michigan. But we have no money, and no gas to do that with, as well as no place to stay for the night. Lord, please, for the sake of my children, and for Your great and mighty name, please bless us with the things we need, which is food, and shelter, and fuel. I don't know how You'll bless us tonight, but I leave that in Your loving and capable hands."

Just then she felt a nudge in her heart.

"Fuel your car," a still, small voice said to her.

But her mind rejected its summons.

"I have no money, Lord," her thoughts replied, almost seeming to refute the claims of faith she'd just demonstrated.

"Fuel your car," came the urging again.

Jenna nodded slightly, almost by instinct, and then obeyed the voice that was speaking to her. She had no idea how they would pay for their gas, but if God wanted her to fill her tank, one way or another, they would get the gas they needed. So she climbed out, lifted the nozzle off the pump, and stuck it in the gas tank. But, much to her shock and surprise, as soon as she pressed the button to select the 86 octane gas, the pump went nuts. Its TV like display screen began to flash "Winner!" over and over again almost as though she'd just hit the jackpot in Vegas. A moment later the PA system crackled to life.

"Pump nine, I'm sorry for the inconvenience. Please wait one moment while we figure out what's the matter," came a voice over the PA system.

Jenna only nodded. She wasn't sure what'd just happened, or what to think about her current situation. Deciding to trust God entirely in this, she replaced the nozzle, and then stood there patiently for what seemed like forever as she waited on the attendant to tell her what to do next. Eventually the PA crackled to life again.

"Pump nine, please hang up your nozzle and report to the service counter. Pump nine, please hang up your nozzle and report to the service counter, please."

Jenna's heart leapt with fear. Had she gotten in trouble? Did they know she didn't have any money? Was she about to be arrested and separated from her children? Not wanting to incriminate herself, she did as she was told and stepped inside. As soon as she did she locked eyes with one of the cashiers who cocked an eyebrow slightly.

"Are you from pump nine?" they asked.

"I am," replied Jenna sheepishly.

The cashier nodded.

"Just a moment, please. The manager will be right out," they said.

Jenna's mind began to reel.

"The manager!?" she thought in horror.

Just then two men walked out of the back office and approached the counter. One of them brushed the cashier aside and began working with the terminal for a few moments. He soon turned to an envelope in his hands and began digging through it, eventually pulling several items out of it. Upon opening them the man's brow went up.

"Wow, are you the fortunate one today," he said.

"What do you mean?" asked Jenna.

"Well, you're a lucky winner in our surprise giveaway. According to this, not only do you get a free tank of gas, but you also get a hundred dollars cash, and a certificate for a free room and dinner at the Budget Inn just down the street."

Jenna looked at him in shock!

"Dinner and a hotel room!?" she said in amazement.

"Yeah, as well as a hundred dollars of spending cash, and a tank of free gas."

It was at this moment that a river of tears broke forth from Jenna's eyes as she cried with joy, and then hugged one of the men, whom she later discovered was the store manager, before backing up apologetically and smiling sheepishly. The man laughed.

"If only all of my customers were as grateful as you," he chuckled.

"Well, shall we get the picture?" asked the other man.

The manager nodded, grabbed $100 out of the till, and then, with all of her prize items in hand, stood with Jenna, and the other man, to get their picture taken. After this Jenna refueled her car, climbed in, and immediately headed down the road towards the local hotel, tears still streaming down her face. Once again God had come through for her, and in ways she'd never expected.

"You are so wonderful, Lord, and yet I am so unworthy of Your grace."

"You are more than worthy, My child," came a still, small voice within her heart.

"But why me, Lord?"

"Because I love you."

Jenna smiled.

"Thank you, Lord."

Jenna awoke the next morning to a brilliant beam of glistening sunlight coming through the window of her hotel room that felt warm on her face. She looked up to see her little daughter, Emma, standing by the window looking at the city outside as Brad sat on the edge of the bed trying to rub the sleep from his eyes.

"Good morning," she said happily.

But Emma appeared conflicted, and didn't say anything. She merely continued staring out the window as she seemed lost in thought. This moved Jenna's heart, causing her to get out of bed, and walk over to the window, where she sat down next to Emma, and wrapped her arms around the little girl, drawing her close.

"What's the matter, sweetie?" she asked.

"I miss my friends already. We won't be going back to our school anymore, will we?" asked Emma, sadness clearly echoing in her voice.

This poked at Jenna's heart too.

"No, I'm afraid not. But, wherever God is taking us, we need to trust Him, and know that it's for our own good."

Little Emma nodded, even though it was clear to her mother that she still wasn't quite able to wrap her mind around what was happening. Then again, neither was Jenna.

"I'm hungry," grumbled Brad through groggy, sleep soaked eyes.

Jenna grinned. She'd just spent her first waking moments in a wonderful mother daughter moment only to have it immediately spoiled by the bottomless stomach of a ten year old boy. She wondered if she'd done the same thing to her parents at that age.

"Get dressed and we can go downstairs for breakfast," she said.

The young boy looked at her for a moment like she was crazy, and then slowly dragged himself off the bed and into the bathroom. He reemerged ten minutes later fully dressed, but still looking half dead to the world. Emma then went in next followed by Jenna who took the least amount of time getting ready, despite needing far more personal time to get herself back to normal in the mornings. But, at this point, looking a hundred percent was the least of her concerns. They soon gathered all their things, made their way to the lobby, gobbled down the continental breakfast that was being offered there to all the hotel guests, and then checked out of their room.

The night before, shortly after checking in, they'd been treated to a beautiful, five star meal far more ritzy and expensive than Jenna would have ever been willing to pay for, even when she was working a good job, and was flush with cash. But, in the end, when you have a loving

Heavenly Father who's looking out for you, even a five star restaurant isn't out of budget. And to say that the meal was divine would be an understatement. Even so it was now time to go. After finishing their breakfast, they loaded their meager belongings into their car, and headed down the road. They then drove for nearly six hours straight, even traveling through Las Vegas as they headed east.

The massive hotels and other buildings along the strip, visible on their right as they passed by it on Interstate 15, intrigued the two children. But these were merely passing flights of interest as they continued on their way. They soon passed Nellis Air Force Base and eventually made their way out into the Moapa Valley. This is where brown, sandy hills turned into green and brown speckled desert that stretched on for miles and miles in every direction with barely a respite in sight. There were no houses, or towns, or anything to speak of anywhere. Just miles and miles of sun scorched land, and seemingly endless, boring desert. And, if Jenna was finding the repeating miles of monotony to be mind numbing, she knew the kids were feeling it even more. But, much to her surprise, rather than hearing whining and complaining coming from the back seat, she instead heard singing.

This brought a smile to everyone's faces, and continued on like this for several hours with one new song following another. In Jenna's mind it was like church on four wheels. They eventually made a quick pit stop in Mesquite, Nevada along the way to allow everyone to get out and stretch their legs. Afterwards they forged on as fast, and as far as their old car would take them before allowing even it to rest for a time. As the day drew on towards evening the brown and green speckled desert slowly gave way to dusty green hills covered in small evergreen shrubs. Eventually they reached Richfield, Utah, a city of intriguing contrasts and breathtaking views, and found that it presented them with an unusual irony that was clearly visible to any travelers that were passing by there. On one side of the highway was brown, dusty desert hills covered in sun burnt scrub grass. Not a house, a road, or even a single tree was visible as far as the eye could see.

It was desert through and through. Yet, on the other side, spreading all the way out to the horizon, were trees and lush green grass interspersed between dusty blacktop roads and colorful houses of every shape and size laid out in neat little rows on tidy little parkways that pierced through the glorious green carpet around them like little black pencil lines. This lush green, well ordered magnificence was, in turn, back-dropped by blue and emerald green mountains covered in thick, lavish layers of botanical life, and gently watered from above by lite, whimsical rain clouds that gave it an almost mystical garden of Eden feel, despite its location deep in the desert. It was as though the highway was the dividing line between the rich greenery of life, and the barren desert dryness of death.

Stray too far to one side and you entered a land of lifelessness. But go the other way and you'd find the fullness of life, rich and abounding. After getting some food and gas at one of the local stations, they continued on until they reached Silverthrone before stopping for the night. However, despite all the distance they'd covered, Jenna now faced a new dilemma. They had enough money to fill their tank. But not enough for a hotel, or even a cheap roadside dive. Realizing that it'd be pointless to get a hotel room if they didn't have any gas to continue on, she filled her tank, pulled off to the side, parked, and then sat there quietly as her two kids played in the back seat. Not knowing what to do, she began to pray.

"Lord, we need Your help again. You know our situation, and You know the predicament we're in. We need a place to stay for the night, and we're once again out of money with no way that I can see to go on. Please, if You wish for us to continue, I ask You, give us a place to stay for the night. You've already blessed us greatly on this journey so far. So I pray, please, bless us again," she prayed.

She'd no more than finished her sentence when a knock came at her window causing her to jump in surprise. Standing outside was a gentleman dressed in a suit that was holding a pair of hotel key cards in his hand. She immediately locked the doors and then rolled the window down a crack just enough to talk to him.

"Yes? Can I help you?" she asked.

"Are you Barton?" he asked.

Jenna was surprised at this.

"Yeah," she said, unsure of what more to say.

"You're heading east, right?"

Jenna's eyes grew wider.

"Yeah," she said slowly, not sure how to take this.

The man nervously fingered the two key cards in his hand.

"Well, last night God gave me a dream, and told me that you would be coming through here, and would need some place to stay for the night, and said to wait for you here. So here you are, and here I am, and...well, this is for you," he said awkwardly.

He then pressed the key cards through the window.

"These are the keys to the hotel room God told me to get for you. Um, I've arranged for dinner for you and your children and...well, um, God said He'd handle the rest."

The man gulped nervously, turned, headed over to his truck, and drove away. Jenna rolled the window up and then stared at the key cards. They came from a strange guy in the middle of a town she'd never been too and she didn't know what to make of it.

"Do not fear. It is safe for you to go there, for God has provided you a room, and has sent me to stand guard so that you may sleep safely tonight," came a voice to her right.

Jenna nearly leapt through the roof of the car in shock and surprise as she turned and noticed that there was a very large, muscular young man sitting next to her in the passenger's seat. His clothes and skin were bright white and seemed to have a shining, almost iridescent glow to them. Even stranger was the fact that he'd somehow gotten into the car despite the doors and windows all being closed and locked.

"Mama, there's an angel in the car," said Emma.

"Who-who are you!?" cried Jenna.

The man cocked an eyebrow slightly and gave her a look of muted incredulity at the fact that her daughter had already figured it out, and yet she hadn't.

"I am sent of God to be your guardian for the evening. Evil forces wish to harm you. But I am here to ensure that they are kept from achieving their dark purpose," he said.

This was a new one for Jenna. She'd seen God move in some pretty amazing ways already, but to have an angel sitting next to her in her own car was new.

"The room is 117. It's waiting for you and your children," he said.

Jenna nodded slightly, started the car, and then made her way, with the angel's guiding, to the local La Quinta Inn. But, before they got there, they came across a police blockade. As she pulled up to it, several cops in swat gear motioned for her to roll down her window. She complied.

"Driver's license and registration, please," said one of the policemen.

Jenna quickly pulled them out, and handed them to the officer, who looked over her papers, and then the car.

"Number of occupants?" he asked.

"Three," she replied.

She was hoping that, if the man next to her wasn't who he said he was, the cops would quickly catch on. At that point she could then explain her situation, and possibly get herself out of this mess. But, to her surprise, the cop acted as though he couldn't see the man sitting next to her in the front seat. And, in plain fact, he couldn't. All he could see was Jenna and her two children. The cop pursed his lips slightly as he studied the clearly nervous mother. Thankfully, he perceived this as just normal anxiety rather than any kind of guilt.

"What's your destination, ma'am?" he asked.

"The La Quinta Inn just ahead," she said.

The cop studied Jenna for several moments, trying to determine if he needed to speak with her in more depth.

"Everything alright, ma'am?" he eventually asked.

Jenna nodded.

"Yes, we've been driving all day, and I'm really tired, and you guys surprised me. I wasn't expecting this," she replied.

The cop sighed.

"Yeah, sorry about that, ma'am. We've searching for some thugs that are on the loose in this area and causing mayhem. We've just not exactly sure where they are right now. You can proceed to your hotel, but please be sure not to let anyone in, or answer your door until we give the all clear. I wouldn't want you to get hurt."

"Understood, officer," replied Jenna.

He then handed her papers back to her, and sent her on her way. As she pulled away she looked over at her mysterious passenger and studied him with interest. Clearly he was who he said he was. This completely took away all of her fear, and also made her extremely curious to know more about him. Yet he didn't seem interested in answering any of her questions, although he appeared to know what she wanted to ask. So she said nothing. They soon arrived at the hotel, went into their room, and put down their bags. It was at this point that she noticed that the man wasn't with them anymore. She stepped outside to see where he'd gone and found him standing guard by the door, arms crossed, and face severe and frightening, as though waiting for the worst.

"Aren't you coming in?" she asked.

"My place is here. I will ensure that you remain safe tonight," he said.

Jenna smiled, and said, "Thank you."

"No," said the angel sternly. "Thank God. He is why I am here."

Jenna smiled.

"I will," she said kindly.

The next morning Jenna awoke to find her two children still sleeping soundly in the bed next to her. She soon got up, washed herself, and then came out and turned on the TV to catch the morning news. To her surprise there was a report on about a manhunt that'd gone on throughout the night and had, much to her relief, ended only a few hours earlier. But what intrigued her the most was when the news reporter ran a clip showing the angel, who'd been guarding her door during the night, standing over two angry, hog tied suspects that were laying on the ground at his feet in the middle of a local parking lot. She smiled.

"When you provide security, Lord, You *really* provide security," she chuckled.

She then walked over to the door and leaned out. As expected the angel was gone. Apparently his work was done, and as such he'd moved on to his next assignment. She thanked God for His blessing of protection during the night, and then went about waking the children and getting them ready for the next part of their trip. They soon checked out of the hotel, and made their way out of the sleepy little desert town where they continued on their way along Interstate 70, eventually coming into the city of Denver, nestled deep in the Colorado mountains. Part way through the city they found themselves forced to switch off of Interstate 70 and onto 76.

Jenna had wanted to stay on I-70 all the way through the city, keeping to a familiar highway until she was into a less congested area. But traffic had forced her to keep left, ultimately resulting in her being shifted onto Interstate 76. The only thing that kept her from panicking over this rather inconvenient redirection was the signs that pointed to the fact that they were still going east. As long as they were doing that, she was fine. They could always make course corrections later on if they found themselves going the wrong way. Eventually Highway 76 led them out into the beautiful green countryside of Colorado on the other side of Denver. But, to both their intrigue, and surprise, whereas the west side of Denver had been very mountainous and hilly, the eastern side was flat, and almost washboard in appearance, with wide open, nearly treeless expanses of fertile farmland stretching out as far as the eye could see in every direction.

But even this soon faded away and, by the time they'd gotten to Wiggins, the only hills and valleys that remained were man made. Everything else was postcard flat. Even the scattered islands of forested trees seemed like tiny lines of green on the distant horizon, as though they'd been etched into the flawless blue sky with a thin green pen. But, as they passed Lexington and Kearney, the land quickly filled with trees. Not all at once, as there were still many, many wide open and treeless expanses to be seen. But the islands of trees, which had once been a rare site, were now quickly growing in number. Eventually, by the time they reached Grand Island, the land was lush, full and rich with trees, rivers, wetlands and wildlife. It'd been like going from the deserts of Egypt to the Garden of Eden, and all within a few hundred miles.

However, by this point in time Jenna again found herself back in the same position as before, once more low on gas, and in need of a way to fill up again. But, if experience had taught her anything by now, it was that God was always with her and, one way or another, He'd provide her with everything she needed to continue on. Pulling off at exit 312, she turned and headed north on highway 34 into Grand Island in search of fuel. But those plans soon got sidetracked by the overflowing bladders of her children. Because of this she was forced to go in search of bathrooms, and soon pulled into the local Super Saver grocery. It wasn't where she wanted to stop, but it'd work for now. Plus, stopping here gave her the added advantage of being able to buy all of them something to snack on that wasn't expensive, gas station food.

It wouldn't be much, but it'd at least be something. She soon pulled into a spot directly across from a very beautiful, and expensive, light silvery gray SUV and parked. She then stared at it for several moments as she thought back to the days when life was good, and money was abundant. Back then she could've owned a car like that if she'd wanted. But those days were gone now and, despite a distant longing for a return to those times, she was content with what she presently had because, unlike that long ago time in her life, God was with her now and, even in the deepest, darkest pits of poverty, she was richer than she'd ever been when times were good! And, if poverty was where God wanted her, then that's where she wanted to be! Because, to her, it was better to be poor in this life and rich in Heaven, than rich in this life and a pauper up there.

She and her two kids then got out and made their way into the store. It didn't take long for them to find the bathrooms and avail themselves of them. They then wandered around the store for several minutes, searching casually for something to eat that would fit within their very meager budget. Eventually they found something that, much to her delight, was the right price, and it was on sale! They soon made their way to the front, checked out, and headed for the car. And, even though their dinner for that night would consist of nothing more than peanut butter crackers, and a couple of sodas, it was still a blessing to them. But, just as they began to approach their car, they immediately noticed two things that were different than before. The first was that the expensive SUV was gone, and the second was that there was now several strange green papers sticking up from their wiper blade and flapping gently in the afternoon breeze.

At first Jenna thought they were merely junk fliers meant to convince people to buy things they neither needed, nor could afford. But, as she got closer to the car, her mind slowly began to wrap itself around what she was actually seeing. Those weren't fliers. They were hundred dollar bills!! Her heart nearly leapt out of her chest in surprise at this. She immediately sprinted to the car, briefly forgetting about her two children, and snatched them out from under the wiper. They were indeed hundred dollar bills! Three of them in fact! Jenna's eyes went wide in amazement as she held the money in her hand. She then clutched them to her chest and began crying.

"Thank you, Lord. Thank you!" she exclaimed.

"Mama! Mama! What'cha got?" asked Emma.

"Manna from heaven, honey."

"Cool! Can we eat it?" replied the boy.

This drew a smile from his mother.

"No, Brad, this isn't the kind you can eat," she chuckled. She then looked to the sky, and said, "Thank you, Lord, for blessing us yet again. I don't know what to say, or why You're even doing this, as I'm not worthy. But...I thank You for this manna, and I pray that we can use it in a way that is befitting of You."

"Amen!" said little Emma.

The next morning, after a good night's rest at a local hotel, and a healthy breakfast, Jenna fueled her car, and set off again for Michigan. By now they were well over halfway there, and really only had two more major legs of the journey to go. So, with a pocket full of money, which was more than enough to get them there with some to spare, Jenna felt confident that the rest of the journey would be easy. But, she was sadly mistaken. As they passed a small town just a few miles outside of Iowa City, the unthinkable happened. The car begin to make a very strange and unusual sound, and not a good one at that. Suddenly a bang and a thud filled her ears as the left rear wheel assembly came apart like a bomb, sending debris all over the road.

"Oh God, no! NOOOOOO!" she cried as she tried to keep control of the car as it disintegrated under her.

It soon careened towards the highway median as her children began screaming at the top of their lungs from the back seat. Jenna did her best to maintain some semblance of control over the car, but it would do her little good. A moment later the vehicle shuttered violently as it impacted a guard rail along the edge of the median, causing it to leap into the air briefly before coming down hard, and to an abrupt, almost immediate halt. When everything came to a stop Jenna sat in her seat shocked, and yet amazed that she was unhurt. The only sound now was the still gentle growl of the engine. She put the car in park, turned off the engine, and then climbed out. She briefly inspected herself and, finding nothing wrong, she opened the back door and got her two children out. She then wasted no time checking them for injuries, and was pleased to find that they were unhurt.

"Are you alright?" she asked.

The two children nodded, but said nothing, clearly terrified from the experience. A moment later a policeman came bounding over to her, clearly anxious to see to her well being. But then something odd happened. He shooed her away as though she were merely an annoying bystander.

"Excuse me, ma'am, but you'll have to step back! I need to get to the passengers in this vehicle," he barked.

"Um, we *are* the passengers. That's our car," she said.

The officer looked at them for a moment like she was nuts, and then shooed them to the side as he made his way over to the driver's side front and rear doors which he found, much to his surprise, open and the occupants gone. He then looked at Jenna and her two kids, and then the car, then Jenna, and finally the car again. He scratched his head in utter amazement and disbelief.

The officer then pointed a thumb at the vehicle, and asked, "This is *your* car!?"

"Yes, officer. That's ours. Or, what's left of it."

The officer tilted his head back slightly and scratched his head. By all rights, given the condition of the vehicle, they should've had at least a few cuts and bruises. Yet there they stood without so much as a scratch on them.

"Are you alright, ma'am?" he asked.

"We're fine," replied Jenna.

Just then the echo of sirens could be heard in the distance.

"Alright, stay right there, ma'am. I want the ambulance to check you out before we do anything else."

Jenna nodded. About a minute later a fire truck, an ambulance, and two more patrol cars pulled up to the accident, they too expecting to find the worst. They even shooed Jenna and her kids away just like the first officer had, thinking they were just curious bystanders as well. Yet they were shocked when the officer told them she was the driver.

"But...but, how!? Nobody should have walked away from that in one piece!" protested one of the firemen.

"Divine intervention. It's the only explanation," said another.

"Wow, talk about guardian angels," said the first fireman.

Jenna considered that the understatement of the day. After being checked out by the ambulance people, she was then set aside while the police and firemen worked to clear the road. Eventually a tow truck came by and picked up the remnants of her car and hauled it into town, with them riding in the passenger seat all the way. But, as they made the short trip to town, Jenna looked back at the car and sighed. It'd already brought them so far, and now it was nothing but a wreck.

"What now, Lord? That was our only way to reach Michigan," she thought.

But she heard no answer. She knew this had to be for a reason. She just couldn't figure out what that was just yet. The tow truck soon pulled into the parking lot of a local garage where they climbed out as the driver talked with one of the mechanics. Eventually he got back into his truck, expertly dropped the mangled vehicle into one of the empty parking spots, and then handed Jenna the towing bill. She quietly paid it, and then turned her attention to the mechanic, who was now inspecting what remained of her car. Given the look on his face, the news wouldn't be good.

"Can it be fixed?" she asked apprehensively.

"Well, I hate to say it, but no. It's bad enough that you pretty much dropped the entire rear end on the ground. But, to make matters worse, you also snapped the frame, probably when you made that spectacular nose dive into the median that the tow driver told me about. I'm actually surprised you walked away from that alive, to be honest. Either way, she's not going anywhere ever again. She's as cooked a goose as you're gonna get."

A look of dejected sadness grew across Jenna's face.

"So it's a total loss?" she asked.

"I'm afraid so, ma'am," said the mechanic.

She now felt even more disappointed and sad. The mechanic felt bad for Jenna, realizing she probably had little if any money, and now had no car either. He then looked at the crinkled hood and shook his head. He wished he could do something for her, but there was nothing that could be done. At least, not without spending a fortune that she clearly didn't have. But, just then, as he began walking away, something caught his eye. He paused for a moment, not wanting to believe what he was seeing. Eventually he reached over and gently pried open the mangled hood. What he found underneath made his eyes grow three sizes bigger.

"Gerd! Get out here!" he shouted.

An older mechanic soon came trotting out to the car.

"Yeah, what's....whoa," he said upon seeing what the other mechanic was looking at. "Is that..." he began, still in utter shock.

"I think it is, which means we're looking at the sleeper of the century."

"Sleeper?" asked Jenna curiously.

"Yeah, in automotive terms a 'sleeper' is a car that looks normal on the outside, but has some serious muscle under the hood. What makes yours a sleeper is this engine. It's a 1973 Oldsmobile model W-43, 455ci Experimental, which is one of the most sought after, and rarest muscle car engines out there."

Jenna looked at him in confusion. This sounded like something her late husband always liked talking about.

"Okaaaaaay, but what does that do for me?"

"Lady, you're sitting on a gold mine. In fact, tell ya what. I'll make you a deal. $500 and I'll take the car off your hands no questions asked."

Jenna blinked, unsure of what to do. Cars were her husband's thing. So she didn't understand any of this. However, this brief flash of confusion made it appear to the two men that she was holding out for more money. Seeing this, and fearing that she might bolt and take the engine with her, as well as a potential windfall profit, Gerd, the older mechanic, grabbed the young man by the arm.

"One second, ma'am," he said apologetically.

Jenna then watched as the two men walked away, and seemed to argue vigorously over something. Most likely her car. She almost wondered if the one mechanic wasn't trying to convince the other to scrap the whole idea and just send her packing. A minute later the two men returned.

"Tell you what. My partner and I have been discussing this, and we realize that you drive a hard bargain. So we're willing to give you a thousand," said the younger man.

"Davis," hissed Gerd.

But Jenna didn't appear willing to budge. But it wasn't because she was holding out for the best price. She honestly had no idea what was going on. And, like before, the two men mistook her confusion for someone who was pushing a hard bargain.

"$1500?" asked Gerd.

"Two grand," retorted Davis.

"Three grand."

"Alright, five grand, and not a dime more," snapped Davis.

Jenna stared at the two men in confusion, still completely uncertain of what was happening. If they were serious, and really wanted to give her that much money, she could certainly use it. In fact, it'd be far more than she needed, and would easily get them a nice car and plenty of gas for the remainder of the trip. Or, at the very least, bus tickets to wherever they needed to go. She was hoping for a new car, but would settle for anything by now. However, before she could say anything, the old man spoke up.

"Ma'am, since my partner here won't offer you a fair price for that engine, I'll give you seventy five hundred out the door. Deal?" he asked.

Jenna appeared to think this over for a bit, and then nodded.

"Okay, I can do that," she said hesitantly. "But what do I do about a car? I obviously can't drive this one anymore."

The two men looked at each other briefly before retreating across the lot where they discussed this for several moments. Eventually they returned.

"Ma'am, we've both come to a decision about your car that I believe you'll like. You obviously need a new one, and we need that engine. So here's what we're gonna do. I have a buddy of mine down at the local dealership who owes me a favor. So I'm going to talk to him about getting you a good used car, and everything you need for it, and we'll pay for it in exchange for your engine. That way you'll have the new car that you need, and we'll get our engine. Sound like a deal?" said Davis.

Jenna smiled happily at this.

"I'll take it."

The dealer looked at Davis incredulously.

"You're not serious, are you?" he said in disbelief.

"Come on, man. You owe me bigtime, and I'm sitting on a gold mine here!"

"Yeah, but I can't cut her a deal that sweet! I'd lose money!" protested the dealer.

"Are you seriously going to bolt on me now? Dude, you owe me huge. Time to pay up, and I ain't joking," said Davis firmly.

The dealer leaned back in his chair and thought about this for a bit. Finally he sighed.

"Fine, I'll do it, but after this we're even, got it?"

"Deal!" said Davis.

"Alright. Mrs. Barton, if you would, please," said the dealer, motioning to a chair in front of his desk.

Jenna sat down anxiously, not entirely certain what to make of the whole situation.

"Okay, here's the deal. I have a car on my lot that I can sell you for what it cost me, which should be what they've agreed to pay you for your car. But don't worry about that. I'll sort out that detail with them later. For now, we just need to get you into a new car. That'll be the easy part. Just sign some paperwork and we can get you on your way. As far as money for this purchase goes, Davis and Gerd have already covered that," said the dealer.

"What about insurance?" asked Jenna.

"Well, thanks to our wonderful governor, and the new bill they passed a few months ago, whenever you buy a car in our state, you automatically get thirty days of provisional full coverage insurance as part of your purchase price, which should be enough to get you to your destination, at which point you can get your own from there."

"Oh, well, then we're covered," said Jenna in surprise.

"You are. Now, all we have to do is complete the necessary paperwork, and I can get you your title and keys."

Jenna then quietly complied, and signed everything that was placed before her, before handing them back to the dealer.

"I've signed everything you've asked," she said.

"Good, then that completes all of our paperwork for you."

"What about my plate?" asked Jenna.

"I got that covered too."

Jenna nodded.

"Thank you."

The dealer smiled.

"You're welcome. Now, one moment while I go get your new car."

He then disappeared into the back, returning a few minutes later with a freshly printed title, and everything else she needed for the car. The problem was, up to this point, she hadn't seen her new car, as she'd done everything sight unseen. Even so, she trusted that, whatever God gave her as a replacement, it would be good enough.

"Just so you know, I don't have your keys with me at the moment, because I asked one of the guys to pull the car around front for you. So your keys will be waiting for you out there, along with your new car, when it arrives," said the dealer.

"Which car is it?" asked Jenna.

Davis pointed out the front window, and said, "It's right there."

Jenna looked out the front window, but didn't initially see anything. However, not more than a moment later, a completely immaculate, deep burgundy red Buick Regal pulled into view. Jenna's jaw nearly hit the floor.

"That's your new car, ma'am. I even took the liberty of bringing all your stuff with me, so we can pack it in your trunk, and get you on your way," said Davis.

"Wow," was all the words Jenna could muster.

The other men laughed.

"That was worth selling us that engine, wasn't it?" asked Davis.

Jenna nodded.

"Uh-huh."

She then went outside and began inspecting the car as the dealer put her paperwork in the glove box, and Davis put her belongings in the trunk. She and her children then got into the car and drove away, still stunned that God had given them such an incredibly nice upgrade from their old wreck of a car. As Jenna pulled away from the dealership she still couldn't quite get her mind around the fact that she'd just been given a nearly brand new car for free. So, no matter how much she tried, it still didn't feel like it was hers. In fact, it felt like she was driving someone else's baby. She soon pulled into a local gas station and up to the pump. But, as she filled up her tank, she faced a new problem. Being in Iowa City, she was at a crossroads. If she continued down Interstate 80 she'd be able to enter Michigan from the south. However, if she went north along 380 to Cedar Rapids, she could enter via the Upper Peninsula. She mulled this over and over in her mind, but couldn't determine which way God was sending her.

"Lord, where do You want us to go? I don't know which way to turn," she prayed.

Just then the wind picked up, and a piece of paper came sailing out of nowhere and adhered itself to her windshield. She walked over and, pealing it off the windshield, studied it with interest. It was a travel flier for the town of Newberry, located in the Upper Peninsula of Michigan. An eyebrow went up slightly.

"Is this where you want us to go, Lord?" she asked.

Just then another breeze snatched it from her fingers and slapped it on the windshield again in the same place it'd landed before. Jenna blinked slightly.

"Message received, Lord," she replied.

She then took the flier off the windshield again, tucked it into her purse, paid for her gas, and then climbed into the car. Once inside she pulled out the little flier and studied it. On the back she found a map that showed where to find the little city, and even how to get there from at least four different directions. So, having her marching orders, she made her way onto the highway and headed north. They then drove for another few hours before stopping for the night in Cedar Rapids. The next day they made good time, turning north through Dubuque, and then Madison, Wisconsin, and finally up into Appleton where they stayed for the night. But now they had another issue. The money they'd been given in Grand Island had nearly run out. The last two days of gas, hotel stays, and meals had done the most damage to it. At this point there was only enough to top off their tank one last time, after which they would be broke again.

Thankfully, though, they weren't that far from their final destination. So Jenna filled her tank one last time, and then set out towards upper Michigan, continuing north through Green Bay, and out onto route 41, on which they stayed for several hours until they reached Menominee, Michigan. After passing through the city, they switched to route 35 and followed it through Escanaba, Gladstone, and then the Shingleton state forest to Manistique. However, their journey wasn't without at least a few postcard stops, as they paused several times along the way to enjoy the beautiful, natural wonders and sights around them, which provided a very fun and exciting distraction for the children. Living in Los Angeles, they'd rarely had the opportunity to be this close to nature, and yet here they were, deep in the thick of it, enjoying every minute of it.

They even got to see some Elk along the way, which was a special treat for both children. Even Jenna was enjoying it, despite her city upbringing. It was as though, through this journey, and their time in God's creation, He was slowly and gently deprogramming her of the life she'd come from, and preparing her for what lay ahead. Eventually, though, the trip they'd started on, all those days before, finally came to an end as the city of Newberry came into view before them. First it was merely a road sign, and then a placard, which eventually became the outskirts of a quiet little town, deep in the heart of Northern Michigan.

But, as Jenna, and her children, were looking on in wonder at the world around them, a still small voice tugged at Jenna's heart.

"Look to your left," it said.

Jenna quietly obeyed and, as soon as she did, she noticed an old bed and breakfast just up ahead alongside the highway. But, what was most interesting was, right next to it, standing at the end of the main driveway, was a sweet old lady who seemed to be beckoning for her to pull over. So Jenna did, although she wasn't sure what for. Upon pulling into the driveway, she lowered her window, and was greeted by the bright, shining, beaming face of Margaret, the owner of the Shepherd's Bed and Breakfast.

"Are you Jenna Barton?" she asked.

Jenna did a shocked double take.

"I am. How'd you know?" she asked.

Margaret grinned.

"God told me. He said you were coming. He sent you here for a new beginning, and a new life, leaving behind everything that once encumbered you in the place that is now your former home," she said kindly.

Jenna wasn't sure why, but at that moment all the anxiety, fear, pressure, and weight that'd been on her shoulders for the past two years just suddenly melted away, which brought on a fountain of tears. But not tears of sadness. Instead, they were tears of joy.

"Mama, why are you crying?" asked Brad.

"Because I'm happy," bawled Jenna.

Margaret turned her eyes to heaven, and said, "Praise you, Lord, for this wonderful sister, and praise You, Lord, for bringing her safely to us by Your divine power and will." She then turned her eyes back to Jenna, and said, "Come inside, dear. We have much to talk about, and much to prepare you for, as God has chosen you for something great, and He has chosen me as the means by which to bring you to that destiny."

"Amen," replied Jenna with a smile.

And with that she pulled her car into the parking lot. Upon getting out she took a deep, long breath of fresh air, and soaked in the lovely fragrance of nature all around her. And, for the first time in her entire life, she truly felt free of her past, and all of the tears it'd brought to her. What lay ahead of her now were many good days of living and serving the Lord in her new home, in a sleepy little town in Northern Michigan.

The End